PRAISE FOR *MURDER IN MENNEFER*

"In *Murder in Mennefer*, Al Sirois rebuilds the ancient capital of Lower Egypt in painstaking detail and wills it to leap directly off the page in thirteen-year-old Imhotep's tragic tale of murder, loss, deception, and duty. A must read for lovers of mystery, history, and intrigue!"

— Frank Morelli, author of *Breaking News* and *On the Way to Birdland*

"In Egypt so long ago that the pyramids had not yet been built, thirteen-year-old Imhotep dreams of adventure, but his father's mysterious death instead brings responsibilities and danger. He has to grow up fast, from dealing with enemies and false friends to supporting his family, and even experiencing first love. There are cobras, potions, a young prince—and everywhere the Eye of Wadjet is watching. Al Sirois has crafted a thrilling tale grounded in ancient history but pitch-perfect for contemporary readers."

— Valerie Nieman, author of *In the Lonely Backwater*

"In the ancient Egyptian city of Mennefer during the time of cruel and benevolent gods, thirteen-year-old Imhotep's hopes of becoming a healer are dashed after the sudden, apparent accidental death of his father, a successful builder, forcing the family into penury. *Murder in Mennefer* is not only a mystery but a coming of age story plus an enlightening look into everyday life along the Nile: its customs, food, tomb building, and even the making of mummies. Highly recommended."

— Don Swaim, author of *The Assassination of Ambrose Bierce: A Love Story*

"Writing a believable genius is harder than it looks but A. L. Sirois' *Murder in Mennefer* pulls it off. His ancient Egyptian protagonist is Imhotep, future designer of the first pyramid; here he's just a bright young man until his father's death forces him to prove himself. He does. This was a fun Y/A mystery with great historical detail."

— Fraser Sherman, author of the steampunk novel *Questionable Minds*

"A tense, suspense-filled novel that digs deep into popular Egyptology. What couldn't Imhotep do? He built pyramids, practiced medicine, became deified, but as a teenager he solved crimes. A feast for literary YA historical fiction and crime-solving minds alike that also begs the question, what can't author Sirois do?"

— Chris Bauer, novelist, *Max Fend Maximum Risk* series, *Blessid Trauma Crime Scene Cleaner*s series

MURDER IN MENNEFER

A. L. Sirois

Fitzroy Books

Published by Fitzroy Books
An imprint of
Regal House Publishing, LLC
Raleigh, NC 27605

https://fitzroybooks.com

ISBN -13 (paperback): 9781646034727
ISBN -13 (epub): 9781646034734
Library of Congress Control Number: 2023942957

All efforts were made to determine the copyright holders and obtain
their permissions in any circumstance where copyrighted material was
used. The publisher apologizes if any errors were made during this
process, or if any omissions occurred. If noted, please contact the
publisher and all efforts will be made to incorporate permissions in
future editions.

Cover images and design by © C. B. Royal

 Regal House Publishing, LLC
https://regalhousepublishing.com

Printed in the United States of America

To my wife, Grace Marcus, without whom this book would not have been written.

1

With a grunt, Imhotep hoisted his heavy cloth bag onto the deck of the cargo boat. Hands on his bony hips, feet splayed, he felt as buoyant as the boat rocking on the gentle swell of the river. The Nile snaked around the white-walled city, holding Mennefer in its green embrace. Except for excursions to building sites with his father, Imhotep had seen little else of the world. Today, all that would change.

Last night, unable to sleep, he had crammed a few more poultices and papyrus scrolls into his already bulging sack. *Who knows what dangers or discoveries await?* Then, still restless, he paced the flat rooftop of his home, once again scanning the sky for a sign in the stars.

Though he and his younger brother, Sebhot, often made light of their mother's propensity to fret, Imhotep couldn't help feeling nervous. Omens and portents, messages from the gods, filled the air. One would be foolish to ignore them. All week he had prayed to Heka, the god of magic, and ibis-headed Thoth, who had revealed to men the arts of writing and healing, to beg for a sign promising good fortune for his voyage. But neither made a response until yesterday, when Imhotep had come to the riverside before dawn to pray once more.

That morning, Sopdet, the brilliant star that had ushered in the new year and the annual inundation a scant month ago, had been visible above the horizon for only a few breaths before the light of Lord Re's glorious chariot obscured it. Not even the fishermen were yet at their nets, though smoke from cooking fires threaded the early morning sky, warning away the other stars as Lord Re took possession of the firmament. Disturbed by Imhotep's approach, a duck burst up from the reeds. And then from nowhere a hawk dropped down on the smaller bird, seizing it in its sharp talons, bearing it off with a harsh scream.

Imhotep had shivered in the cool morning air. Birds...surely a sign from Thoth. *But did it mean that I'm the hawk? Or the hapless duck?*

That's the problem with omens. They mean one thing when you see them and another once the foretold event occurs.

But this morning on their way to the dock his mother, Ankh-kherdu, known to all as Kherry, spotted a big white bird with a black head taking flight from a clump of reeds. Imhotep's heart soared along with the ibis. Another sign, indisputably from Thoth! Now he looked up at the sky, where Lord Re had burned off the early morning clouds. A silky wind promised smooth sailing.

He closed his eyes.

> *Many thanks to you, O Thoth, who sees all things,*
> *and seeing understands,*
> *and understanding has the power to disclose*
> *and to give explanation.*
> *The sacred symbols of the cosmic elements*
> *have you hidden away...keeping sure silence,*
> *that every younger age of cosmic time might seek for them.*
> *And now I go to seek them, O Thoth. Watch over me!*

"Early, eh?" Thuya jostled Imhotep, tipping him off balance. "Hey!"

Thuya laughed. "Better get used to it. The Nile is not always so gentle." At fifteen, only two years older than he, his friend Thuya already earned his wages as a sailor, respected enough by the captain to secure a berth for Imhotep. "You'll see, when we reach the cataract."

"Tep! Help me aboard!" Sebhot, somewhat shorter than Imhotep and heavy enough to be considered plump, waved from the dock.

"Nay, I'll come ashore," said Imhotep. Sebhot would have his own chance for adventure when he reached thirteen next year. Imhotep fastened his tunic tighter around his narrow waist and scrambled onto the dock.

"Two months is a long time. I'll miss you, Tep."

Imhotep clasped Sebhot's chubby arms and swallowed hard. "I'll miss you, too, and the City of the White Wall." At Ankh-kherdu's raised eyebrow, he added, "Yes, Mother, and you and Father as well. But Thuya assures me we'll be back in time for the Festival of Thoth. I would not miss that."

Sebhot's voice dropped to a murmur so that their mother wouldn't hear them speaking over the river breezes. "But you won't miss Father's shop, eh?"

Imhotep's smile grew broader. "Not *so* much, no. I have no heart for business, like you." This was the only cause of dissent between father and son: Kaneferw wished his eldest son to take over the master apprenticeship at the atelier, even though he already employed a talented assistant named Ahmose. *Perhaps, after my return, Father will have changed his heart. Or I will find mine. Much can happen in two months.* He glanced upriver for a glimpse of his father's boat. Kaneferw was returning from the Fayum, where he was supervising construction of a retreat for the king, and had promised to be back in time to see Imhotep off.

Thuya left his three crewmates stacking goods in the vessel's bow. Expertly shifting his weight to the swaying of the boat, he approached the knot of people above him on the quayside. "All is in order, we should leave soon," he called up to them. "Lord Re climbs the sky and won't wait for us." He rubbed his hands together. "You'll enjoy the voyage, Tep! The Island of the Elephant is a fascinating place too. So many exotic people there, with birds and beasts and plants the likes of which you have never seen. The markets! Ah, my friend, you may think of ivory and gold and animal skins, and they are there; but the scent of the fruits and vegetables!" He closed his eyes and swayed back and forth, nostrils flaring. "Precious oils, incense…I swear by Isis, you could live on the air alone. I can't wait to be there again."

Imhotep grinned at him. Just downstream of the First Cataract, the island boasted the mightiest fort on the river, protecting the southernmost border of the Two Lands where it met northernmost Nubia. The island's location made it a natural cargo transfer point for river trade. Imhotep fairly danced with eagerness to be off on this, his first extended trip away from home. "As soon as my father comes, Thuya, we will say our prayers and I will be ready."

A few paces away, Kherry spoke fretfully to old Chancellor Pepi, a longtime family friend. Imhotep overheard her say, "My husband should have been here by now."

Imhotep exchanged a knowing glance with his brother. *There she goes again. Always worrying,* their tented brows said.

The chancellor adjusted his pectoral necklace with a thin hand. He placed his other on Kherry's arm. "Patience, my dear. It is more than a day's journey from the Fayum, remember."

"But Father has been traveling more than a day," said Seb-hot to Imhotep. He squinted at the rising sun. "He would have started at first light yesterday, or before, and by my reckoning, given the distance to the Fayum, his boat should be arriving at any moment."

Kaneferw, whose official title, Master of Public Works, made him part architect, part builder, and part bureaucrat, had sworn on Horus to be present when Imhotep set out. And he was not a man to break a promise, especially to his offspring.

Imhotep cast his gaze upriver, willing his father's boat to appear. Perhaps, because he'd been addressing his prayers this day all to Thoth, the river felt slighted and was delaying his return.

He recited softly, "Hail to thee, O Nile, who gives life to the Two Lands. Watering the orchards created by Re, to cause all the cattle to live, you give the earth to drink, inexhaustible one."

At his elbow, a dry-as-papyrus voice finished, "'You cause all the creations of Ptah to prosper.'"

"Master!" Imhotep clasped Hau's papery forearms. The teacher's advanced age of sixty-five years, a rarity in the Two Lands, added to his reputation as a sage and healer. "An honor. I did not expect you—"

"—to stir my bones at this hour?" Hau chuckled dryly. "I'm not so lethargic as I appear. And you are not so humble as *you* appear."

Imhotep flushed.

"Don't worry. Not everyone can read your heart as do I." He ran his hand over Imhotep's shorn head. "It must be only yesterday when you wore the sidelock."

"Two months, actually." Imhotep grinned ruefully. Along with the sidelock, he'd also lost most of his foreskin on the day of his ritual shaving, and to the same barber. His groin gave him a twinge at the memory.

And although he took pride in his large, shapely skull, without the sidelock to hide at least some of them, his acne blemishes now seemed more visible than ever.

"So as a skinny boy you leave us, but as a man will you return."

"One hopes." Imhotep had spent more time studying poultices and spells with Hau than pleased his father. "You have a broad heart," Kaneferw often said to his eldest son, folding his arms and frowning. "Too broad! You can never give all your attention to one thing."

Imhotep blinked at the river, scanning for his father's boat. *There are so many skills to learn, so many fascinating things to know. How can a man stay pinned to just one in his life?*

"Be sure to bring me specimens of herbs and medicinal plants you find in the south." Hau rubbed his hands like a fly eager to dine. "And note their effects, my boy. Speak to any healer you meet! Ask questions! I'm hopeful you will find something better able to reduce the pain of a headache than riverwort leaves."

And with the help of the gods something that works on my be-damned blemishes, Imhotep said to himself.

Hau rambled on about riverwort, but Imhotep stopped paying attention to the raspy voice when a familiar craft rounded the river bend. "Mother!" He pointed to the approaching riverboat. A good thirty paces long and nearly five paces wide, made of bundles of reeds lashed together with ropes and caulked with pitch, the vessel approached with sail furled. Eighteen rowers moved in unison, propelling it over the river's swells toward the quay.

Kherry clasped her hands. "Oh, thank the gods. He comes at last." Excitement flickered among the onlookers as the vessel drew nearer.

"Father hires the finest boats," Sebhot said with the same satisfied tone he used after he'd solved a complicated mathematical problem. Of the two brothers, Sebhot had much the better head for figures. From an early age he'd displayed a facility with numbers and amazed his family and friends by knowing the dates of all the many religious festivals. Imhotep clapped him on the shoulder. Before Lord Re's flaming boat rose much further into the sky, Imhotep would be off. He could scarcely keep from crowing out loud like the hawk he'd seen yesterday. *Its cry was my joy at seeing Father approach. All is well.*

As the boat drew nearer, Imhotep spied the captain at the bow, and the master apprentice's slave, Odji, busy hauling sacks and bundles on the deck. Even from this distance, the boy's strength was apparent. No doubt that could be attributed to Odji's endless duties as a slave. Or perhaps it was consolation from the gods for a life spent in captivity. Even with all his talents, Imhotep felt a sting of envy for Odji's physical prowess.

Sebhot stood on his toes. "Where's Father?"

"Sheltering from Lord Re's fire, perhaps."

"Can you see him under the canopy, Tep?"

"Nay, but they're heading in. Let's go!" Imhotep bolted down the quay to meet the vessel, Sebhot at his heels.

The boat was near enough now for Imhotep to see Odji kneel to fasten his master Ahmose's sandals. Ahmose, Kaneferw's chief apprentice, leaned his bulk against the mast. His left arm was bound close to his body by linen cloth.

"What's happened to Ahmose, poor fellow?" Kherry joined her sons.

"A wound?" ventured Chancellor Pepi.

"I see...no...visible blood." Hau held up his palm while he caught his breath and coughed once. "Mayhap he's broken a bone."

Imhotep balanced on the lip of the stone jetty, eager to greet his father, receive his blessing, and be on his way.

His own way, not his father's. Kaneferw had showed him how to swim in the Nile, how to draw, and even how to read and write, before Imhotep's formal education began at the temple of Ptah in the center of the city. In the evenings his father taught Imhotep the names of the stars as they revealed themselves in the deepening sky, and told him of the gods living in them, igniting Imhotep's imagination.

The only cloud in the clear sky of his life was Kaneferw's expectation that he work in the atelier. At Kaneferw's insistence, Imhotep had apprenticed with a stonecutter, learning to translate his drawings to the rock itself. But the stonecutter lost patience with Imhotep's lack of strength and told him to go home.

"It's true, you do not have a stonecutter's brawn," Kaneferw had acknowledged, eyeing his son's scrawny form, "but it is necessary for you to experience all phases of tomb-building." It satisfied Imhotep's endless curiosity to know such things, even though he preferred studying herbs and healing spells with Hau. Kaneferw disdained the ragged old healer. "Advanced years do not necessarily make for high status among men, my son," he'd said more than once.

"Look at you—as tall as a man but thin as a stalk of papyrus. What woman will want to marry a stork?" He nudged his eldest son in the ribs. "The answer, I tell you, is this: if the stork is wealthy and can hold his head up among men, any woman will want him."

"Let Sebhot take my place, let me do as I will. I will not shame you."

"I did not say you would. True, yes, your brother has the makings of a clever merchant." Kaneferw smiled. "You on the other hand…have the makings of a true architect, a builder of temples."

Imhotep had felt trapped by the words, stuck in the atelier amid dry-as-dust papyrus rolls covered with endless drawings of tombs for the wealthy. He tried to explain. "It is the *world* I wish to learn of, Father. The stars, the seasons…the colors in a spray of water. What are they? From whence do they come? And why? Why does the Nile flood when Sopdet comes visible again in the month of Ahket? Why are things as they are? Might they be different? What if they were? I would know these things."

"What is the end of it?" His father had slapped the drawing table with a straight edge. "Like everyone, my son, you will eventually go to the Beautiful West. Now, think: will you go with a heart full of useless knowledge, or will you go with a family who will honor your name and keep you alive through their prayers?"

"Father!" he called now to the figure reclining under the canopy. "Hail, Father!" he shouted as the boat slid into place. Then he saw Kaneferw, his face a ghostly mask, his body shrouded in linen, his limbs as motionless as stone.

2

The image of the hawk and the duck flashed into Imhotep's heart. His legs went weak, but he willed himself to stay upright, gripping Sebhot's shoulder and his mother's hand. An oarsman leaped nimbly out of the boat and tied its painter to a mooring post. Behind him, four rowers lifted the pallet holding Kaneferw's body, their faces sad and gray. Water lapped calmly at the sides of the quay as they placed Kaneferw's litter on the sunbaked stones. Kherry, white-faced, sank to her knees and threw her arms around the shrouded form. Sebhot sobbed. Imhotep clamped his lips to stop their trembling and held his body rigid lest it crumple like a reed under an elephant's foot. *Beloved Father...*

Although his mother's sorrowful wails pierced the din, they did not stop the sailors loading and unloading their vessels, nor prevent the merchants from trading and selling. The life of the City of the White Walls marched on, even as Imhotep's halted.

He released Sebhot when Odji scrambled onto the quay. The slave shot a helpless look at Imhotep but remained silent, then turned to assist his master off the boat. When Ahmose, looking older than his thirty years, lost his footing, Odji grasped him by his injured arm. Ahmose winced. "Clumsy Kushite! A curse on your mother!" He ceased shouting when he saw the stricken faces of those who waited for him on the quay, but the scowl did not leave his own.

"What has happened?" Imhotep seized Ahmose by his shoulders, eliciting another grimace of pain. "Speak."

"An accident, young master. A terrible misfortune." Ahmose ignored the gathering knot of onlookers and kept his reddened eyes on Imhotep. "Two days ago, we were on the site studying the east wall. It had sunk perhaps the length of a finger and had tilted from true. We realized it had to be torn down to make the footing sturdier. We squatted there, your father, Kagemni the overseer, and I, studying the plans, discussing how best to proceed." Ahmose closed his eyes. "And the wall…the wall collapsed. I twisted away. Kagemni flung himself to one side. Your…your father did not escape."

"But you did." Imhotep released Ahmose. "Could you not help him?"

"I tried." Ahmose cradled his injured arm. "But a stone fell on me as I scrambled back. By the time the other workers got there, it was too late." He drew a shuddering breath. "It is a great sorrow."

Hau bent to inspect Kaneferw's body. After a few moments he looked up at Imhotep somberly. "He has been crushed, as Ahmose says." Imhotep scarcely heard him, imagining the sound of the stones toppling, his father's last cries.

The hand on his shoulder pulled him from his thoughts. Thuya held him in a sorrowful gaze. "May he find endless life in the Beautiful West." He leaned close and spoke rapidly. "Just say the word, Tep, and I will remain here until we can travel together. But my captain is ready to cast off so you must decide quickly."

Imhotep's heart lifted. *Perhaps it is not impossible.* After all, his father had blessed his journey. And, once he had settled his father's affairs, both Sebhot's and their mother's comfort would be assured. He must, of course, honor his father to ensure Kaneferw's *ka* would make its way safely to the West. The preparation of the body, the painting of the tomb. He must decide the most propitious time for burial and how many mourners to hire for the funeral. His mother would rely on him to decide Sebhot's future and—

"Tep?"

His first decision was both the easiest and the hardest. "I cannot leave Mennefer now. Go in peace, Thuya. May the gods watch over you. I will accompany you on your next journey."

"I am sorry I cannot stay to see him placed in his tomb." Thuya held his fist over his heart. "This I pledge: every day will I send prayers to Osiris in your father's name."

"Thank you, my friend."

They clasped forearms. "Till I return, then," said the young sailor.

Imhotep nodded, unable to say more past the lump in his throat. *When you return, I'll likely be the lord of my father's atelier, captured like a river fish in a well.*

He watched his friend slip the painter and step down into the boat. The man at the tiller sang out, and the oarsmen pushed off. Imhotep felt trapped, as if his chest were filled with stones, his feet stuck in thick clay as the tide rolled away.

He swallowed hard. "Odji, fetch a sledge. We'll take my father's body to Merisu." The slave bowed and trotted off.

At the embalmer's name, his mother choked out a wail, and buried her face in the chancellor's chest. Sad-faced, Pepi patted her back. "Come, Kherry. I will escort you home. Your servant Wabet will watch over you."

Hau stood beside his student. "I will share your burden," he declared.

"As will I." Ahmose held up his good arm.

"I do not see Kagemni on the boat," said Imhotep. "He is still on-site?"

"He has remained behind to see what can be done to rebuild the wall, yes. I…I don't think it can be saved, but Kagemni is more than competent. If anyone can do it…"

"Yes."

Standing next to Imhotep, Sebhot wept quietly. Imhotep gently cupped his head. "We must be men now." The younger boy nodded, his eyes clotted with tears.

From over the water, Imhotep heard the rowers raising their voices in thanks to the gods of the Nile for the river's blessings.

"Hail to thee, O Nile, who manifests thyself over us, and comes to give life to the Two Lands."

The very same prayer he had breathed not long ago. Imhotep whispered along with them until his throat closed off his words.

Odji returned with a sledge that he placed next to the pallet. He and Hau carefully transferred Kaneferw's body to the sledge. One-handed, Ahmose took a corner. Hau, Imhotep, and Sebhot gripped the others. Imhotep prayed again: *Thoth, make magic on me that I do not shame my father by dropping his body.*

Then he turned from his dreams and, with the others, bore his father's broken body away.

3

The Place of Purification was not far from the quay, but by the time they arrived Imhotep felt as if he'd trudged ten marches through thick river silt. Now that his father's *ba*, his animating spirit, had departed his body, should Kaneferw's remains not feel lighter?

High mud-brick walls screened the embalmer's huge open-sided tent from the Temple of Ptah. Though hidden from sight and sweetened by the smoke of many censers, no amount of perfume could completely mask the smell of decay wafting from within. Inside, bodies lay in various stages of preparation upon stone slabs. One apprentice washed the body of a child while another, a tall youth, wrapped a corpse in resin-soaked linen.

Merisu the embalmer appeared at the boy's shoulder and elbowed him aside to chide an apprentice. "Watch, Kawab! Learn!" The master dipped his spidery fingers into the ewer brimming with sand-colored powder. "Use this on your hands, eh? So that the resin won't adhere to you while you work at tightening and molding the bandages." His hands flashed around the body, patting and pressing so quickly that his fingers seemed to be living creatures independent of his arms, darting here and there like birds.

When Imhotep, Ahmose, Hau, Sebhot, and Odji set Kaneferw's body on an empty table, Merisu lifted his chin in acknowledgement. "A moment!" he called and turned back to his work.

"Go now," Imhotep told the others. "I will stay with my father."

"We would also stay," said Ahmose.

"No, you have done enough and need your own injuries addressed. Hau, will you please see to Ahmose?"

Ahmose shook his head. "No, Hau, I beg you attend to the young master. I will go to my healer on my way home."

"Hau, I am fine," said Imhotep. "You can be of no further help to my father."

"Very well. Then with your permission I will leave. But first..." Hau dug into his tunic and handed Imhotep a small bundle of sage. "This will help." The old man placed a hand on his shoulder. He whispered, so that only Imhotep could hear him, "The stars say that before your father's tomb is sealed, good fortune will befall you." Then with Ahmose and Odji he departed from the tent.

Sebhot lingered. "I should stay too," he said.

"No...this is my responsibility. Go and comfort our mother."

"Very well." Sebhot walked off, shoulders slumped.

Grateful for Hau's gift, Imhotep crushed the sprigs of sage between his fingers and inhaled the herb's fragrance. He looked around the tent. Dozens of clay jars lined the shelves on one side, the largest on the bottom, smallest at the top. A wood trestle held copper blades, needles, and awls. On another were ranked assorted brushes and pots of pigment. On a separate table to one side were several oddly shaped mummies that Imhotep recognized as baboons and ibises destined to be buried as votive offerings during Thoth's festival.

Merisu hobbled over on his bandy legs. He lifted the edge of the shroud. "Ah, Kaneferw. I recognize the master. What a pity." He sighed. "He built my brother's mastaba. You are his son?"

Imhotep nodded, unable to speak around the knot in his throat.

"May the gods receive him with joy, may his heart balance the scales of Ma'at." As Merisu stripped the body, Imhotep quailed at the dark blood sticking to his father's skull and staining the linen shroud.

He had studied wounds with Hau; but those were all of

strangers, people whose lives, loves, and joys he did not know. He winced as Merisu straightened Kaneferw's left arm and leg, each broken in multiple places. Just above the wrist on the right arm, a sharp spur of bone jutted from the flesh. To see his father so still, so torn and damaged! Kaneferw, with his hands as rough as a laborer's, had always preferred the building site to the drawing table; he relished the actual construction of his designs, the inspection of materials and the sizing of stones. When he wasn't working, Kaneferw loved to hunt game birds or swim the Nile, swift as an eel, from bank to bank where it narrowed. They often raced each other, Imhotep's slender form arrowing through the water behind his father. "Someday you'll pass me," Kaneferw had promised.

Now he has left me behind forever. Imhotep clutched his father's cold hand, its fingers waxy and stiff. He fought back tears.

"I will not entrust your esteemed father to an apprentice," Merisu said quietly. "Be assured I myself will wash him with palm wine and waters from the Nile."

"Many thanks, Merisu."

"But first, I must finish that one." He nodded toward the next slab, on which Imhotep saw a boy no older than he. The boy's abdomen was sliced lengthwise, displaying the internal organs. Imhotep noted the groove in the polished sandstone that channeled leaking fluids from the body. Merisu pulled several clay jars from nearby shelves.

Even in the depths of bereavement, Imhotep's curiosity demanded satisfaction, and he was thankful for the distraction.

"Curious, eh?" Merisu regarded him for a moment with his small, bright eyes. "As you wish."

Imhotep stood transfixed as the embalmer carefully removed many lengths of glistening intestine and deposited them in the largest jar. He knew that all the body's organs would be entombed with the deceased. Merisu squinted into the cavity. With a few strokes of a knife, he freed a fleshy mass, the color of brick.

"What is that?" Imhotep blurted out.

Merisu paused. "I have heard it said you are Hau's student. Is this true?"

Imhotep nodded, his eyes still fastened on the wobbly flesh. "Come here."

He approached the table, steeling himself against the thick odor.

"This, my boy, is the liver. Imseti, son of Horus, will watch over it in the West."

Imhotep noted its triangular shape, divided into two lobes. *Perhaps one for each side of the body? But for what purpose?* He must ask Hau. "He is young, he has no injuries I can see. What happened to him?"

"No need to whisper, boy," Merisu boomed as he slid the liver into a jar marked with prayers to Imseti. "Poor Sekwaskhet can't hear you. A sickness in his belly. See? His abdomen is swollen."

Imhotep studied the body as dispassionately as he could, as Hau had taught him. *Do not allow yourself to be sickened or moved to pity by the wounds.*

"Sekwaskhet took to his bed, but the pain became agonizing, and he expired some weeks after first complaining of it. It was the wasting disease, the one that creates strange growths in the body. The healers could do nothing."

Imhotep nodded slowly. *Hau has spoken of poisonous sacs that grow within.* He stared into the bloody body cavity. *One never knows when the hand of Anubis will pluck one's ba.*

Wiping his hands on his soiled tunic, Merisu reached inside Sekwaskhet and drew forth a misshapen whitish mass. "Here it is." Imhotep recoiled, not from the sight or smell, but from the cold fact that a knot no bigger than a quince could kill someone. "This too goes into the tomb. Though it ended his life, it is the work of the gods and must be preserved." Only one jar now remained empty.

Slowly, reverently, Merisu once more slipped his hands into

Sekwaskhet's chest and cupped a wedge of flesh the size of his palm without pulling it from its wet red nest. "Sekwaskhet's heart." Imhotep's own heart lurched. He knew that the source of Sekwaskhet's thoughts and feelings also held his fate. After death, Ma'at herself weighed a man's heart against her feather of truth to see if he had lived with honor.

Leaving Sekwaskhet's heart in place to travel to the West with the body, Merisu excised the lungs flanking it. He deposited them in the fourth and final jar, to be blessed and watched over in the tomb by Hapi, deity of the North, Imhotep knew, so the young man could live again in the Fields of Yalu and accompany the Sun on its daily ride.

"Master, a word?" An artisan held his brush aloft over the finely molded cast of a woman.

Merisu wiped his hands once more and limped over to the finishing table. The careful application of resin and linen bandages to the woman's body had perfectly rendered her slender neck, full breasts, and graceful hands. When hardened by the heat of the Two Lands, the linen would become a shell like a beetle's carapace. Protected from corruption, it was painted, as the artist was now doing, making the deceased appear even more lifelike.

Merisu gazed at the painter's work. "Good, good. Except her eyes are a rare green, not brown." He sighed. "A lovely woman, a magistrate's wife. You can be sure her dress will be of the finest linen, threaded with gold, well suited for the company of the gods."

Imhotep drew in a sharp breath. *His father, always so elegant in his best tunic, his shining gold pectoral necklace, gold bands burnishing his arms. But to meet the gods with this poor broken body...* Unable to help himself, he wept over his father's battered form.

As if reading his mind, Merisu murmured, "Fear not, my son. I promise you, after I have prepared Kaneferw for his journey he will appear as you remember."

Imhotep mumbled his thanks and hurried out into the baking sunlight of mid-afternoon, relieved to be free from the miasma of the master embalmer's realm.

Taking deep breaths of fresh air to flush his lungs, he wove his way through Mennefer's crowded byways. He consoled himself with the knowledge that Kaneferw's *ka*, his true, eternal self, would soon consort with his ancestors and the gods, designing and building new monuments and temples in the Beautiful West.

Biting his lips against the pang in his heart, Imhotep entered the rear courtyard of his home. *How strange… Everything here is as it was yesterday.* The dried-grass broom by the door, the pile of broken pottery shards for writing, the fruit ripening on the fig trees.

He stood frozen on the threshold until Momo mewled plaintively. Jumping lightly from the low branches of a fig tree, the cat advanced, tail up, to greet him.

Imhotep knelt and petted her spotted fur, golden in the late afternoon light. "You don't want to go inside either."

Purring, Momo nuzzled his hand, staring at him with eyes the color of jade, and then vaulted back up onto a branch.

Imhotep rose, steeled himself, and entered the house. It took a moment for his eyes to adjust to the dim interior after the brilliant daylight. A single big room comprised the entirety of the ground floor, with a section in the rear curtained off and used by his mother as her sleeping area. In the back room, Wabet hovered over her mistress, serving her a cup of wine and a plate of figs. Sebhot, swollen-eyed, gobbled honey cakes as if they could fill the void left by his father's death. Ahmose's slave, Odji, sat on a low stool at the foot of Kherry's bed, looking uncomfortable.

At Imhotep's questioning look, Odji said, "My master bid me attend to your mother while his arm is being treated."

Imhotep nodded. "Thank you." He took in his mother's

ravaged face. The kohl lining Kherry's eyes now smudged her cheeks, her nose was as bright as the red ocher she put on her lips, and her wig listed to one side.

"You'd best drink that." Imhotep inclined his head toward the wine.

Kherry sobbed and clasped her hands. "I'm so glad you're back."

"I'll take my leave," Odji said, rising. "You are here now, and I must return to my master."

"Thank Ahmose for his kindness," said Imhotep, accompanying Odji to the front door. "And I thank you for yours." Odji bowed his head. "It's nothing. Your father was always good to me."

"Not like Ahmose, I know… He always speaks so harshly to you, calling you lazy."

"Things are as they are," Odji said with a shrug.

"Perhaps. Yet I wish I could let Ahmose know about the lessons I've been giving you, and how hard you practice your reading and writing."

Several months earlier the slave had come to Imhotep begging to be taught his letters so that he could do the same for his sister, Noha, who was a slave in Chancellor Pepi's household. Then brother and sister would be able to keep in touch by sending messages to each other.

Odji blanched. "Please do not tell him! He would beat me for seeking to rise above my station."

"Fear not." Imhotep sighed. *We all live by the gods' whims.*

Ahmose himself should know better, Imhotep thought as he watched Odji trot off. From a lowly porter, Ahmose, who had been orphaned at an early age, had been made an apprentice and given more responsibility, all of which he handled well. Gradually he made himself indispensable to Kaneferw and had been appointed First Assistant, a privileged place in the atelier. Though Ahmose was unfailingly polite and gracious to Kaneferw's family, his condescending treatment of Odji made Imhotep uncomfortable.

After Odji departed, Imhotep returned to his mother's room and sat beside her bed with Sebhot. She pressed his hand between hers. "You have made the arrangements with…with Merisu?"

He nodded.

She closed her eyes. "Then we have twenty-eight days until the funeral. Wabet," she said to her slave, hovering nearby, "you must prepare the roast duck he loves, and salted beef and dried lamb. Fill a chest." Kherry opened her eyes. "No! Two. Have them made by Harkuf the carpenter. Imhotep, you will make ready your father's tomb."

"Of course, Mother."

"Sebhot, when the time comes, order the finest white bread to fill your father's storage chamber. Use the bakers in the Street of Persimmons."

"I will, Mother."

"And the funeral feast. I shall hire two dozen mourners, invite a hundred guests. We'll need a banquet. I want the best for your father, the best—"

"But—" Sebhot frowned.

"What is it?"

"How are we… I mean, what about Father's business? How are we to pay for all this?"

"My sensible son." She smoothed his hair. "Ahmose will see to the shop until Imhotep settles your father's affairs. Your father provided for us." She closed her eyes. "Yes, we'll need funds. Please take care of it, Imhotep."

He rose to do her bidding, but she opened her eyes and put a hand on his arm. "Not now, my son. Tomorrow is soon enough." Kherry sighed. "Stay near while I rest, both of you."

"Yes. Rest, Mother." Imhotep kissed her cheek, as did Sebhot. They sat silently beside the bed until her breathing became deep and regular. Then they rose and left the room. Imhotep drew a curtain across the entry.

They went to the table and sat.

"She is so pale." Sebhot choked back a sob. "Tep, I miss him." Imhotep nodded, tears in his eyes. "As do I. We will miss him more in the days to come. But we must carry on. It is our duty. We are his sons. In the morning you and I will go to the atelier and sort things out." Imhotep tapped his brother's chest. "I will need that clever heart of yours."

Sebhot finally smiled. Imhotep returned the smile. "Then I will see to Father's tomb."

"Poor Father... He had no idea he'd need it this soon."

"None of us did."

Wabet set a plate of olives, onions, and bread in front of Imhotep, along with a jug of beer. "May the gods protect him," the girl murmured.

"Thank you, Wabet." He had not eaten since the early morning but had no desire for food. He lifted the jug.

Wabet tapped the plate. "You should eat. Both of you."

"For my part, I am not hungry." Sebhot sighed and rose to his feet. "I'm going to lie down too, up on the roof. It's cooler there."

"I'll stay with your mother." Wabet tapped Imhotep's plate again. "Try to eat something, eh? Then you too must rest."

"And you, Wabet. We will all need our strength." Imhotep drank the beer. His thoughts tumbled this way and that. He couldn't hold on to them.

Presently he looked up with a start. It had grown dark while he wrestled with his emotions. He poured oil into a shallow pottery lamp, lit it, and found a length of linen to wrap up his uneaten food. Because it was a hot night, he decided to sleep up on the house's flat roof. Fetching his linen bedding from his sleeping area, he took the lamp, went outside and climbed the stairs to the roof. Sebhot was asleep, snoring softly.

Imhotep arranged his bedding, then doused the lamp. Lying down, hands clasped behind his head, he stared at the endlessly twinkling stars that formed the body of beautiful Nut, goddess of the night sky and protector of the dead.

She would watch over his father as he made his way through Duat, the underworld, to the Hall of Two Truths where Anubis would judge whether he had lived a virtuous life and Ma'at would weigh his honor. Imhotep had no doubt that the gods would rule favorably, that his father would be sent on to the blessed realm of Osiris in the Beautiful West.

O my Mother Nut, goddess of night, stretch Yourself over my father that he may be placed among the imperishable stars which are in You, and that he may live on.

Feeling a little better, he rolled over to one side and settled himself for sleep. Unbidden, an image of Thuya's boat came to his heart. He could even see the sunlight sparkling on the waves.

Or perhaps it was merely the stars…

When he awoke, for a brief, strange moment he thought he was still seeing sunlight on the gentle swells of the river. But it was the eastern sky growing bright as Lord Re's chariot approached, bringing dawn to the Two Lands. He sat cross-legged on his bed. *Thuya must be awake as well, breaking his fast; only he is watching the sights along the banks of the Nile unscroll. What buildings and trees is he seeing? Or animals? Are they the same as here or not? How long will it take the ship to go beyond the Two Lands? And what—*

A gentle snore interrupted his reverie. Sebhot lay nearby on his own pallet. Imhotep stood. Sebhot's limbs sprawled in every direction as was usual for him in slumber. *Let him sleep a while longer.*

Halfway down the outside stairs, Imhotep inhaled the delicious aroma of baking bread. That, and the gentle murmur of women's voices, told him that his mother and Wabet were preparing the day's loaves.

Imhotep quietly entered the house to offer his morning prayers at the small altar before heading to the rough stone stairway leading to the basement.

The low ceiling, formed by the flooring overhead, forced

Imhotep to stoop. He grimaced, remembering how he and his father had labored, facing the cramped earthen walls of the cellar with stones. Most people wouldn't have bothered, would have been content merely with smoothing the walls, but Kaneferw insisted on using stone.

It will make this space cooler and more secure, he'd said. Cooler for the amphorae of stored grain and cooking oil, safer for the carved cedar box his father had hidden. The chest held the atelier's profits, as well as the gold bracelets and faience necklaces his parents wore for festivals or on the rare occasions when they went to the palace. *The next "occasion" will be Father's funeral.* Alone in the basement, Imhotep made no attempt to stifle his sobs. He wept as he would not before his mother and brother, and, he believed, as he never would again.

After, he wiped his face with the hem of his tunic. *Behind the third vat from the stairs,* Father had told him. Imhotep sweated and strained to budge the heavy stone amphora. He would not, *would not,* ask for help. He...could...do...this. At last, he wrested it out of the way. Sweaty, smeared with dirt, he crouched down and reached into the dark recess, his fingers serving as his eyes. Something brushed against his palm. *A snake!* As he reared back he smelled sandalwood. He blew out a breath. *Just a frond to keep out the dank.* Scorpions as well as snakes liked to hide in cellars. He stood too quickly and banged his head against the ceiling. Stars swirled around him. He felt a trickle of blood on his bare scalp and thought of his father's head wound.

If I am to take my father's place, I must be fearless.

He groped around behind the amphora until his fingers found the chest. Seizing it with a firm grasp, he carried the cedar box over to the stairs, where the light was marginally better. Imhotep ran his fingers over the lid, wiping dust from the image of Osiris his father had carved into the wood. Carefully, he lifted the lid. Inside, his parents' wedding necklaces nested together, their bracelets circling one another. But everything else was gone. The spices, the silver... Not even a grain of gold remained.

4

Imhotep raced up the stairs. He shook his brother's shoulder. "Seb! Sebhot, wake up!"

Sebhot surfaced from sleep, as always, with agonizing slowness. Imhotep ground his teeth but would say no more until the lazy turtle opened his eyes.

When he did, they instantly went wide. "Ai! Your head—it's bleeding. What in the name of—"

Imhotep clamped a hand over Seb's mouth. In a hurried whisper, he explained his discovery.

Sebhot's reaction was not what he expected. Instead of being shocked or dismayed, Sebhot merely levered himself up on his elbows and sighed. He glanced sheepishly at Imhotep, then looked away.

"Seb? What's the matter with you? I just told you, all of Father's wealth has vanished. Everything except their wedding jewelry. We have been robbed!"

"No, Tep, we haven't been robbed."

Bewildered, Imhotep sat back on his haunches. "What are you talking about?"

"Father *had* no wealth, Tep. Not really."

"I…don't understand."

Sebhot sighed again and sat up on his bedroll. "Father—" he said, then broke off. He licked his lips and started again. "Father was not a poor man."

"No, of course not, we live well."

"Yes. But we could have been living better. The atelier has a good reputation, and Father's work was never less than outstanding."

Imhotep sighed. "I know all of this, Seb."

"He hired the best people, bought the best tools, used the

finest materials in his projects." He raised his eyebrows at Imhotep.

"Yes, yes, of course. What of it?"

"Well, that sort of quality costs money. What Father did... well, he put almost everything he earned right back into the business. He *said* that he was putting some aside, in the basement, in the cedar box. But..."

"But...he didn't." He sighed again. "He just took out what we needed to live on, and to maintain appearances?"

"Yes. I'm afraid that's true."

"And how is it that *you* know all this?"

"Father told me. I'm sorry, Tep," Sebhot said hastily as Imhotep bridled. "I'm sorry, but he had more faith in my business sense than yours. He made me swear on the blood of Isis that I would tell no one."

"Ai-yi-yi-yi. Not even Mother knows this?"

Sebhot merely shook his head.

"Ai-yi-yi. Seb, we have to tell her now."

"I know, I know. I was putting it off, telling her *and* you."

Imhotep growled out a few pungent curses. "We will speak more of this later. Right now I must go look for work if we are to survive as a family."

"Very well." Sebhot went downstairs to get some breakfast. Imhotep followed him but detoured to the small courtyard where the family performed their ablutions. There on a trestle table were the scrapers and the jugs of scented oil used for washing.

Imhotep stripped and wiped oil on himself, then removed it and the dirt with his scraper. He felt his scalp for blood. *Just a trickle.* From his collection of remedies, always kept handy in several small jars, he selected a bit of moss and pressed it on the cut, then rubbed willow paste into the wound to seal it. Around his waist he wrapped the new linen kilt his mother had made, fastening it with a belt of double-sewn linen.

Standing before the polished copper mirror on the wall, Imhotep rimmed his eyes with kohl and painted his brows black.

He had his mother's soft gaze and slim form, but his father's large skull and prominent nose. His mouth, however, was entirely his own. "That means he will speak for himself," his mother had predicted. But what Imhotep had to say, his father rarely wished to hear. "Leave the stars and the spells to the priests," Kaneferw had growled when Imhotep came to him to discuss his desire to learn new ways of healing in the lands to the south. "Charms will not protect a man from Lord Re's fire or the sandstorms that blow from the Red Lands. No, a man needs shelter and a fine resting place. I will not demand you work as an architect, Imhotep; however, neither will I subsidize your travels beyond this season."

But now, thanks to Kaneferw's mishandling of the family finances, they were without funds. *Not a grain of gold left for us.* He groaned softly. *Would that Father had purchased some cows or wheat fields that I could sell. Chancellor Pepi would help me secure a fair price.* He chewed his lip. *No, not yet. First things first. I want to examine the atelier's records. If Father returned money to the business, Seb and I ought to be able to find out how much he put in, and when. I want to get an idea of how often he did that.*

He found Sebhot in the kitchen, gobbling the bread and figs Wabet had set out for them. Imhotep's stomach roiled. He had no appetite. "Finish up, Seb." He lowered his voice. "I would know more of what Father told you, and what he did with the profits. We must sort through the ledgers. Perhaps we can find out where the money *did* go."

Mouth full, Sebhot nodded and licked the residue from his fingers. Before they left, Imhotep carried a bowl of goat's milk into the courtyard for Momo, who shot out from the shadows before it reached the ground and began eagerly lapping.

৵

Despite Sebhot's protests, Imhotep kept up a brisk pace to the workshop, a small building located halfway between their home and the huge temple of Ptah in the middle of Mennefer. By the time they reached the studio, Sebhot was winded. Imhotep, nervous and fidgety, felt as if he himself could walk, nay run, twice as far, just to delay entering.

Marked by a copper handle in the shape of an obelisk, the workshop door opened onto a large room. An enormous drawing table stood in the middle of the chamber. Knotted measuring ropes and rulers hung on either side of the entrance to the library, which housed the shop's architectural scrolls and business records. Imhotep inhaled the familiar scent of ink and papyri, a small comfort for his father's absence. He stiffened his spine and led the way inside. But when he turned around, he found Sebhot standing frozen in the doorway, finger pressed to his lips. Imhotep followed his brother's gaze to the shadow crossing the threshold to the library.

Imhotep flung out his arm in front of Sebhot and tried to keep the tremor from his voice. "Who's there?"

Ahmose bustled into view, stylus in hand, his left arm still in a sling. "Ah! I did not expect you this early in the day."

"Nor we, you." Imhotep brushed past the master apprentice. An oil lamp rested on the library table. Imhotep touched the ceramic base; it was still warm, most of the oil inside used up.

"I was here before first light to make ready the ledgers, young sirs."

And, indeed, the scrolls were neatly laid out, with carved stones at their edges to keep them flat. "You risked the evil night spirits on our behalf?"

Ahmose flushed. "For your father's sake I would ease your way."

"It's fortunate that you did not injure your writing hand," Imhotep said.

"Yes, I was lucky in that regard."

"Have you not broken your fast, then?" Sebhot said. "Shall I fetch you some honey cake?"

"Gods, Seb, is food all you think about?" Imhotep glared at his brother, who glared back, blushing.

"Nay, but many thanks." Ahmose stifled a smile. "The

ledgers are up to date, including the most recent entry for the wages due on…" He cleared his throat. "The last day."

Sebhot leaned over the scroll, took up a stylus, and moistened an ink cake. He began to tick off the entries as he squinted down the columns of figures. Sebhot, Imhotep knew, would diligently chew on the numbers until his eyes failed.

Imhotep beckoned the master apprentice into the workroom. "Ahmose, Father's business is profitable?"

The assistant cleared his throat. "Compared to other builders, yes. But expenses have risen of late, the cost of materials and labor and transport…and, of course, taxes have not gone down. They never do," he said with a sad smile.

The current projects were, as always, laid out on the drawing table. Imhotep saw just two: the royal summerhouse at Fayum and Lord Horemheb's tomb. The designs for the tomb were grand, with three underground rooms—one of them a lavatory, just in case the spirits felt moved—and a special niche for small models of Horemheb's sailing vessels. Boats had been his passion in life.

Imhotep nodded in approval. *By Thoth, such a commission will provide months, maybe years of provisions.* The dark spirit troubling his heart began to release its hold. But first, they must complete the royal summer house in the Fayum. He studied the plans, placing his thumb over the wall that killed his father as if he could erase it. "The wall, Ahmose," he managed to say around the lump in his throat, "what do you think it will take to rebuild?"

The assistant's brow knitted. "I spoke with Kagemni about this before I left to come to Mennefer with your father's body. To rebuild we will need a large order to the stonecutter and another month of wages. All that, I fear, will devour the remainder of the commission paid by King Sanakhe."

"Even so, we can then commence work on Horemheb's tomb."

Ahmose looked stricken. "I did not wish to trouble you

further at this time. But since your father will not be here to oversee the construction, Lord Horemheb has said he may decide to withdraw his commission."

Imhotep felt his stomach fall. *Damn and blast! Father, what have you done to us?* "I believe Father had consulted with Prince Djoser on another commission. What of that?"

"It is true, your honored father did meet with Prince Djoser last month, but I was not present and thereafter Kaneferw said nothing to me about a royal commission. I know no details."

"But surely there are other commissions to be had; my father was much sought after—"

"Aye, but without him presiding over the atelier we have little hope of more work. He was well known and liked and had an easy way with clients. I fear that people will now turn to the studio of Nakht."

"Nakht? He—" Imhotep bit back on the disparaging remark about Nakht's lack of skill as an architect. It was bad luck to speak ill of a blameless person. He stared down at the table, unable to think.

Ahmose finally asked, "Will there be anything else, young master?"

"What of you, Ahmose? We will not be able to pay you, without commissions."

Ahmose would not meet his gaze. "I...too have spoken to Nakht. He is willing to take me on. I would stay here and help rebuild the business, but I cannot afford to work without pay. Times are hard, Imhotep. Jobs are few."

"Yes, I understand. But will your injury allow that?" Imhotep said bitterly.

"I can still draw plans, if not labor on the construction. And it will not stop me from carving an offering for Kaneferw's tomb, nor from overseeing the completion of the summer-house. For those I will forfeit my customary wages."

Abashed, Imhotep picked up a piece of pottery from a nearby trestle table. He drew several characters on the *ostracum* and handed it to Ahmose. "Take this to your healer, or to Hau if you wish. Have him make a new poultice for your arm. That one will not last forever."

"Many thanks, Imhotep." Ahmose held his fist to his chest, then opened the door to the glaring sun of the day.

Imhotep pulled up a stool next to his brother, who was still lost in his calculations. While Sebhot checked the accounts, Imhotep sorted through his father's project records. There were sketches of houses and mastabas, with arrows meeting at angles from the foundation to the roofline to show where the walls joined. Lintels and peaked pediments were carefully drawn in. It had been Kaneferw's custom to include clever little symbols for altars, furnishings, and even occupants. One house had a cat in the courtyard; another, a family asleep on a roof. But other than paid receipts from the quarries and stonecutters for supplies and the granary and brewery for wages, there was nothing in the drawer aside from a sack of pine nuts, which his father loved.

Had loved.

Sebhot laid down his stylus and rubbed his eyes. He had tugged his sidelock hard enough to unravel it. "The additions and subtractions are correct, Tep. The entries are for commissions and payments, for expenditures for labor and materials, for household provisions. Everything seems to be orderly." He shook his head. "Yet there is almost nothing left on which we can live, nothing. A month's worth at best."

Imhotep's heart sank lower. "How can that *be*? I thought the atelier was more successful than that. If he put the profits back into the business, shouldn't there be more to show? There must be some error."

"I'll redo the calculations." Sebhot wielded his stylus as if it were a dagger. "But," he added slyly, "I cannot work on an empty belly."

This was not the time to point out Sebhot had already consumed two meals. Imhotep heaved a sigh. "Very well, I'll fetch you a loaf from the bakery. Would that suffice?"

"And a honey cake?"

"Aye." Imhotep welcomed the chance to stretch his limbs and clear his heart. Outside, he blew out his breath and trotted along the street toward the stall of Rudjet the baker. But despite Lord Re's chariot blazing across the sky, there was a cold knot in his belly. *Enough wages for a month, and no commissions pending. No trace of Father having made an investment in land or livestock. Yet there must be something! Sebhot will find some error. He must! Then he shall have all the honey cakes he can eat.* He sighed. *At least I have an excuse to see Rudjet's daughter, Meresankh. Perhaps she will be assisting her father today.*

But Imhotep arrived at the bakery so flushed that he was certain his blemishes stood out more than usual, and now he hoped she would not be there. He wiped his brow with the hem of his tunic before approaching the open-air stall.

Meresankh was present, arranging loaves for display. She paused as soon as he stopped in front of the racks, her dark eyes radiating sympathy. "Oh, Tep. I'm so sorry to hear of your misfortune. May the gods protect and guide your father."

"Many thanks." Torn between gazing at her lovely face and hiding his own, he asked for several loaves and a honey cake to turn her attention from him. Tall enough to reach the highest shelf, she chose the freshest bread for him.

"The honey cake is yesterday's, I'm afraid." She raised her delicate arched brows in question, and he nodded. *Sebhot will devour it happily enough.*

"But please accept an extra one to sweeten your sorrow, my friend."

He mumbled his thanks and took his leave, savoring both Meresankh's words and the extra honey cake on the way back to the atelier. *All will be well. It must.* Imhotep felt buoyed with every step. *Sebhot, that clever heart, will find a miscalculation. He shall have earned a honey cake and more, by Thoth!* But as soon as he saw Sebhot's woeful countenance, he knew. There were no miscalculations. The family were all but poverty-stricken.

৵

Ankh-kherdu blanched at the news. "I had no idea he was not putting money aside for us," she said faintly. "None, none." She looked reproachfully at her younger son. "You should have told me."

Sebhot coughed and rubbed the back of his neck. "I...I *wanted* to, Mother, truly I did. But Father made me swear not to."

"Always I knew of his ambition for the business," she said, shaking her head. "But I never dreamed he would take it so far."

Imhotep knelt by her chair. "We must reconsider Father's funeral expenses."

His mother shot him a look of outrage. "*That* we will not. I will do what I must to safeguard your father's journey. I can—I *will* barter my silver bracelets, my gold ankh." She touched the delicate charm at her throat, a gift, Imhotep knew, from Kaneferw on their wedding day. He placed his hand over hers. "Not that, Mother. Not yet. I will find a way."

She looked at him with such hope and gratitude, he felt as if he'd been transformed into a strong, capable man. Although he knew that he was not, he must act the part. "Wabet," he called the slave. "Come help Mother to bed."

At that, Kherry's head bowed, her shoulders sagged, and she allowed Wabet to help her to her room.

"Perhaps I can hire my services out to assist shopkeepers with their calculations," Sebhot ventured.

"Perhaps." But Imhotep doubted it. *Not once they learn of our failed circumstances. His skills as a bookkeeper will be suspect.* No. He would speak to Chancellor Pepi about securing Sebhot a position as a temple scribe.

I must find work. And quickly. But first, I must attend to Father's resting place.

On the ferry across the Nile to the City of the Dead, Imhotep opened his sack to check his supplies: several pots of paints; three brushes, along with some figs and onions; and a loaf of bread wrapped in a length of linen.

He looked longingly at the boats on the horizon. If his life had gone according to his expectations, by now he would be well on his way to the First Cataract and Nubia beyond.

As they neared the shore, Imhotep fingered the amulet at his throat and murmured a protective spell.

"Save your prayers, young sir." The ferryman hawked and spat over the side. "Many's the year I have ferried people hither from Mennefer and yon back to it. No ghosts float around at this time of day."

Another passenger, a rangy man with several days' growth of stubble, said, "Not ghosts, perhaps, but devils in the form of the Sons of Atum."

"Eh?" said Imhotep. The Sons, he knew, were southern renegades who denied the superiority of Ptah and all other gods, claiming that Atum was the true creator of the universe, not Ptah or Re. The Sons were sworn enemies of King Sanakhe, who headed Ptah's temple in Mennefer.

"They attempted a raid on the granary at the temple of Ptah," said the man. "Killed a priest!" He shook his head.

"I knew they'd caused some troubles among outlying provinces far from Mennefer," said the ferryman in a grim tone. "But lately, I have heard, they've been active in Heliopolis. It's not good to hear of these terrorists so near Mennefer."

Imhotep bit his lips. Heliopolis was not many marches north of the city.

"You mark me, there'll be worse soon," said the unshaven man darkly. "And you, young sir, may be needing stronger prayers. As will we all."

At the landing Imhotep stepped off onto the shore and set off at a rapid pace toward the tombs.

"Do not dawdle," the ferryman called after him. "Re's own boat settles onto the west, and mine must be back on the eastern shore ere his disappears below the horizon."

Imhotep knew the man was right about ghosts not being out in the daytime. He felt brave enough as he made his way through the ranked tombs toward the site of his father's tomb. By dark, though, the spirits of the dead would be abroad. Most were benign, no doubt, but not all. Some were jealous of the living and desired vengeance. *That is, assuming one believes all the tales of evil spirits.* Though he'd grown up hearing them, Imhotep wasn't sure he did. Nevertheless, there was no point in being reckless about such things. He would not linger here after sunset.

He hurried toward Kaneferw's tomb near a spur of rock. Not as grand as that of a nobleman, his father's mastaba nevertheless contained a resting place for his mummy, and two rooms to store food, furniture, and clothing for the afterlife. Imhotep circled the tomb. Its sloping walls, not quite as tall as he, were made of brick, with decorative niches all around the outside, thirty-two altogether. Imhotep had labored here himself, helping the masons lay the bricks. One especially deep niche would serve as a mortuary altar for visiting mourners once the tomb was sealed for eternity.

Imhotep closed his eyes, as the irony of it sank into his heart—Kaneferw, killed by the very things to which, as Overseer of Works, he had devoted his life: architecture and construction. He frowned and blew out his breath, banishing the melancholy thoughts. *Father should have had the grandest mastaba of all. One that towers over the others, the size of two tombs; no, three— But wait. Wait....*

Why could one not place a smaller mastaba atop a larger one? No one had ever done it, but... The idea immediately captivated him. What a grand structure *that* would make! Expensive, no doubt, but the additional cost would not matter to a nobleman; they were always looking for ways to one-up their peers by constructing ever more elaborate tombs. For that matter, why not erect a third or even a *fourth* mastaba, each one smaller than the last, so that the finished tomb towered into the clear blue sky like a staircase for the gods?

Forgetting his grief for the moment, he took a large piece of broken pottery out of the sack he carried.

With a small stone, he scratched a rude diagram of his idea on the shard. Chewing his lip, he gazed at it. He could see it in his heart's eye, from the side as well.

On another piece of pottery he drew a second sketch:

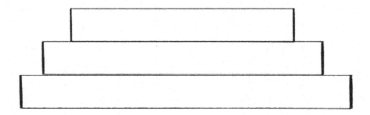

Yes, well worth pondering, but not now; there was much to do. He tucked the shards into his sack. Ducking his head to avoid cracking it on the lintel, he descended the steps into the tomb itself via the door in the western wall. Inside, the floor was littered with dust and bits of stone. The *bas-relief* wall carvings were complete but only three of the four murals had been finished. One portrayed a solemn Kaneferw standing before the throne of Osiris, awaiting his judgment by the scales of Ma'at; another of Kaneferw, stylus in hand, bent over a scroll in his studio. The largest was the family portrait: Imhotep's handsome parents flanked by their sons, Sebhot far thinner than his current self. Imhotep sniffed at his own likeness, which he didn't consider at all flattering. For one thing, it had been executed while he had still been wearing a youth's sidelock. For another, he looked as thin as a stork.

Well, that couldn't be corrected now. He must finish the fourth wall before the funeral. It depicted a robust Kaneferw on a hunt. Imhotep didn't regard himself as much of an artist, but enough of the work was complete that he felt capable of adding the finishing touches: mostly painting in stands of papyrus, adding some color for water, and putting in a few more ducks.

Ample light came in through the door and the ventilation holes leading up through the mastaba above. These would be closed and filled in after construction was completed. Imhotep set to work, pausing only to attend to calls of nature and to wolf down some of the food he had brought.

Painting the reeds turned out to be trickier than he had expected. It wasn't until he found himself with his nose nearly touching the stone, squinting at his work, that he realized the daylight was failing. He would miss the last ferry if he didn't hurry. He packed up his brushes and paints and stepped out of the tomb.

He gasped. A figure hovered behind the mastaba. Prickles of fear spidered up his spine. He clutched his amulet to ward off the ghost and tensed to run.

5

A ghost with a bandaged arm. "Ahmose!"

"Forgive me for startling you." Ahmose pointed down the hillside. "I came to visit my mother's resting place, just over there. I thought to leave an offering at your father's altar as well. I did not expect to find you here."

"That is kind of you, Ahmose, considering the hour."

"Ah yes, wandering spirits."

Imhotep nodded.

"Have you not considered that our misfortunes occurred in the brightest light?" Ahmose drew a small stone carving from the sack slung across his chest.

Imhotep could barely make it out in the fading light. "Is that Osiris?"

"Aye. For protection."

"Perhaps you should keep it for our journey home," Imhotep half-joked. "Come, I will carry your sack to the ferry."

"Nay, my friend Panehsy has rowed me over and waits for me at the bank. I would not trouble you, nor slow you down." Ahmose cocked his head. "On the other hand, we could transport you as well, if you wish."

Imhotep hesitated. If he hurried, he could just make the last ferry and cross the river before full dark. But Ahmose was in no shape to scramble down to the dock, and who knew how fast Panehsy rowed? "It grows dark, Ahmose."

"I will take my chances with the devils, Imhotep. I fear them not."

Imhotep blushed. "I will go, then. I do not wish to cause Mother worry—"

"Good boy."

Imhotep, no longer considering himself a boy, bristled at the "compliment" but said nothing. He nodded curtly and waited until Ahmose turned his back, and then ran, heart pounding, to the ferry, where the ferryman waited impatiently.

He disembarked on the eastern bank just as Lord Re disappeared below the horizon. Murmuring protective charms, Imhotep rushed home, pursued by the night.

A fortnight passed following his encounter with Ahmose at the tomb. In that time, he had by his estimation walked a dozen marches in ever-expanding circles looking for employment— from the docks along the Nile, to Merisu's tent in the heart of Mennefer, to the quarries and breweries in the outlands, even to the farms north of the city. *No work.* Crops had suffered in the drought. With food so scarce and taxes so severe, even the very young, the elderly, and the infirm labored at whatever work could be found. *Thank the gods we have managed to scrape together enough for Father's funeral feast tomorrow. But after that, where will our sustenance come from? How will I provide for Mother and Sebhot, for Wabet? I still have not found a job, nor has Sebhot.* Imhotep's innards churned. How many lectures had Kaneferw given him about financial responsibility? How could his father—advocate of the practical, the prudent path—have been so neglectful of his own responsibilities? How could he have been so careless?

Chancellor Pepi, in whom Imhotep had confided, had little to offer to enlighten him. "Our parents are not always the people we think they are," he said. "I am sorry to hear of your money woes, Imhotep. Difficult though it may be, your father's contracts must be honored lest his spirit be unable to proceed to the West. And of course, the law requires it." He shrugged. "I, too, am puzzled and dismayed by his failure to provide for his family. Knowing him as I did, I am certain he never meant to leave you in this position." He placed a sympathetic hand on Imhotep's arm. "Perhaps I can be of some financial assistance—"

Imhotep shook his head. "I thank you, honored sir, but it

would only shift my burden to one side without relieving me of it."

Following his meeting with Pepi, Imhotep trudged slowly home, where he lingered in the punishing heat of the courtyard rather than bear more disappointing tidings to his mother. He collapsed under a fig tree's listless leaves and rubbed his aching calves.

Weary now, he closed his eyes, conjuring Thoth, hoping for a sign. A feathery kiss brushed his cheek. His eyes flew open. Momo's stared back. She licked the salty perspiration from his upper lip, tapped at him with her paw, and padded away, inside the house. He shuffled after her.

At the table, Kherry nibbled the meal Wabet had placed before them while Sebhot devoured his food. Wabet scurried in with another bowl when she spotted Imhotep, but he waved it away. "None for me, thank you."

"But you ate nothing this morning," the girl said reprovingly.

"I dined earlier with Hau." He hadn't, but he didn't wish to deplete their larder, nor give cause for concern. Wabet's cheeks looked so hollow that he was sure she, too, was forfeiting her portions to stretch their provisions.

Wabet squinted at him in suspicion and pursed her lips but kept silent. Sebhot ate doggedly, as if in a trance.

"And what magical elixir had Hau for you?" Kherry inquired. "Some donkey dung for good luck? A special plant for prosperity?" She had taken up Kaneferw's disdain for the healer, as if to keep faith with her deceased husband.

Imhotep ground his teeth at his mother's bitter tone. *How can she not see that the magic truly heals?*

Sebhot offered him a baleful look. "Have you any news for us, then, Tep?"

"Let me wash up, Seb. We'll talk after."

Momo followed him into the courtyard, where he peeled off his tunic, wet his hands, and dipped into a pot of *swabu*. He worked the paste into a lather and scrubbed his skin until it stung, then used a curved scraper made from bone to remove it. His flesh, sparer now than ever, showed his ribs as a ladder of bony ridges, his legs as spindly as those of an ibis. His face was a spotted landscape. *Perhaps in Kush or Nubia I would find the proper alchemy to banish these damned blemishes.* He shook his tunic to get rid of the red dust and draped it around his body. *When will I have my chance?*

As soberly as he could, he assessed his situation. With proper learning he could earn his living as a healer. He'd build an apothecary, conjuring up poultices and unguents not only for the apparent disfigurement or broken bone but for the hidden sicknesses that poisoned the blood or grew foul lumps like those inside the dead boy at Merisu's. Hadn't Hau scried a vision of Imhotep, brow furrowed, working over an open wound? And had Hau not also predicted that Imhotep's opportunity would manifest before his father's tomb was sealed? That would occur soon, yet it still seemed an eternity away. *Blessed Lord Thoth,* he begged, *send me a sign.* He spun around when the pile of ostraca rattled, in time to see Momo prance away, a small snake dangling from her mouth.

At sunset, Imhotep joined his mother and Sebhot on the roof. The western sky was stained with a red glow. Kherry alternately fluttered and crumpled a palm frond, Sebhot perched on a stool next to her chair. Imhotep straddled the parapet.

They sat in silence as darkness deepened around them. Soon the brighter stars showed their sparkling selves, to the east and far above. The friendly glow of oil lamps glittered in nearby windows, and appealing odors wafted past as families prepared their evening meals.

Imhotep paced the length of the roof, staring out into the night, hands clasped tightly behind his back. Even in the failing light he saw his mother's gaze follow him.

"Hau cannot make magic in an instant, Mother. He consulted the gods and assures me they will intervene. One needs faith."

"If your father were alive, he could have procured you a fine apprenticeship," Kherry lamented.

Imhotep sighed without replying. *If my father were alive, there would have been no need! Besides, I was apprenticed to the stonecutter and failed because I am not strong. Can she see only my limitations and not my gifts?*

Before dawn on the day of Kaneferw's funeral, Imhotep lit three tapers—one to bless his father's spirit, one to protect his mother and brother, one to give him strength.

Then for hours, as the funeral procession walked to the river and crossed via ferry to the tomb, Imhotep prayed for the safety of Kaneferw's *ka* as it journeyed to the Beautiful West.

True to his word, Merisu had sculpted Kaneferw's body so well that even the slight downturn of his left eyebrow had been retained. The hard resin-soaked linen had been painted in lifelike colors, and then dressed in Kaneferw's best tunic. The gold collar he wore for formal occasions glittered in the early morning air.

Ankh-kherdu, her features smeared with ashes, stood at the head of the bier. Tears mottled her face. Her two sisters followed immediately behind her, weeping and wailing, their garments torn and their hair streaming. Because there were so few close female relatives, three professional mourners had been hired, and their sorrowful cries were even louder than those of Kherry and her sisters. Behind them Sebhot and Wabet carried food and clothing for Kaneferw's journey.

Outside the mastaba, a priest, masked as Anubis and dressed in a leopard-skin mantle, sprinkled the body with lilac-scented water and waved incense over it as he chanted prayers. Then he and Imhotep maneuvered Kaneferw's bandaged form into standing position, facing south. When Imhotep staggered, Odji stepped forward and steadied him. Imhotep felt his face flame red, but he muttered his thanks. The priest touched the mummy's mouth, ears, eyes, and nose with a sacred flint, thus enabling Kaneferw to eat, see, smell, and breathe in his next life. With trembling limbs, muscles burning, cursing his physical weakness, Imhotep helped the priest carry his father's body into the tomb. Once inside the crypt, the burden in his heart felt far greater than the one in his arms.

They laid the body in the sarcophagus, which the priest then purified by rubbing it with milk and salt. Kherry entered, wailing in grief, and, with a weeping Sebhot, placed jars of food beside the body. Imhotep slipped his arm around his mother's shoulders, pulled Sebhot to his chest, and held them tightly as the priest made the final offering, the ceremonial foreleg of a freshly butchered cow.

Imhotep led his family back into daylight and then, speaking as his father for the first and only time, addressed the mourners. "Oh, you who live and exist, who love life and hate death, who shall pass by this tomb, so shall you offer to me that which is in your hands. If there is nothing in your hands, you shall speak thus. 'A thousand of bread and beer, of oxen and geese, of alabaster and linen—a thousand of all good and pure things, for the venerated Kaneferw.'"

The mourners did as they were bidden, sobbing as they filed away.

Chancellor Pepi clasped Imhotep's hand. "May he be blessed in death as he was in life."

"Osiris willing," Imhotep answered. He kissed his mother and brother. "Go with the chancellor. I want a few moments alone."

They didn't argue. He slipped back inside the dim chamber to wait with his father's mummy. His bones felt fused, his flesh cold, his heart as still and hard as the stone walls, his thoughts as blank. He knelt beside the coffin; a cry of anguish escaped his lips. Composing himself, he stepped out into the harsh sunshine. Tomorrow masons would fill the tomb passages with rocks, sealing it forever. He climbed back to the sunshine, feeling as if his own *ka* had been left behind, trapped within Kaneferw's sepulcher.

༃

At home, Imhotep fled to the roof to escape the cacophony of music, wails, and blessings from the guests overflowing the house at the funeral feast. He scanned the courtyard for Meresankh. He had glimpsed her twice before, accompanying her father to deliver the bread, and then on the ferry back from the tomb. He had not spoken to her—what, after all, would he say?—but it was soothing simply to rest his eyes on her lovely countenance. When Sebhot carried a pair of stools to the shade of the fig tree, Imhotep tried to catch his brother's eye. Sebhot, however, didn't look up, just stood dolefully as Wabet escorted Kherry into the shade.

The sound of footsteps on the stairs to the roof made him lift his head. Ahmose approached.

"Ah! There you are." Imhotep frowned at the intrusion, but Ahmose kept a respectful distance. "I am glad to find you alone. May I have a word?"

Imhotep sighed, feeling he could not bear any more bad news. "Can it not wait?"

"Unfortunately, no. But perhaps what I say will be helpful. You will pardon my presumption, Imhotep, but I know your predicament and thought only to, well—"

"Yes, Ahmose?"

Ahmose fiddled with his pectoral necklace. "I have a great friend named Ni-Ka-Re. He has charge of a well-regarded butcher shop—"

"Yes?"

"I, uh, may be able to secure you an apprenticeship there. It's hard work, true, but these are difficult times. Ni-Ka-Re has many supplicants, but I prevailed upon him to wait until I had spoken to you and—"

Ahmose said more, but Imhotep heard little of it, envisioning himself spattered with gore, dismembering a carcass. Hau's prophecy flashed into his heart. *I see you standing over an open wound.* He felt the blood drain from his face and grasped the parapet for balance. *As a butcher, not as a healer! Is this the gods' idea of a joke?*

Seeing his distress, Ahmose said, "Nay, of course, it is beneath you, Imhotep. Pray forget I mentioned it. I meant only to be of assistance." He turned away.

Imhotep gazed down into the courtyard at his mother's ravaged face, his brother's swollen eyes.

"Ahmose, wait."

"Yes, young master?"

"I am grateful. Tell your friend..." He swallowed hard and forced the words from his throat. "Tell Ni-Ka-Re I will speak with him."

6

The stench greeted Imhotep long before he reached the gate to the abattoir, where a boy no older than Sebhot but far thinner dumped a basket of reeking entrails into a woven reed container nearly as tall as himself.

"I am to report to Ni-Ka-Re," Imhotep managed, trying not to inhale.

The boy grinned, showing gaps in his white teeth. He thrust a thumb at his scrawny chest. "Dhuti."

"Imhotep."

"This way, my friend." Dhuti led him on a circuitous route, dodging around the ranks of crude tables that were no more than planks on trestles, where workers variously skinned, quartered, chopped, and trimmed carcasses. Despite the endless heat parching the land, the ground here was muddy, sticky with blood from the slaughtered cattle.

Under a palm-frond roof, a sturdy man of perhaps twenty-five years cleaved what looked to be a lamb's carcass in two. He had a broad chest and powerful arms. A small whip was tucked into his belt. A hulking young assistant eviscerated the entrails and scooped the pile into a basket, then, with the axe he was handed, quartered the animal.

"Not bad, Tesh-Pa," said the big man.

The youth smirked. "Thank you, Master Ni-Ka-Re."

The man took back the axe. "But not good, either."

Dhuti snickered, earning an evil look from Tesh-Pa. "Master," Dhuti addressed the man, "here is Imhotep."

Ni-Ka-Re wiped a film of blood from the copper axe. He studied Imhotep as if he were appraising a suspect cut of beef. He tossed the axe to Imhotep, who managed to grab it with both hands and held it, wobbly, at mid-hilt to maintain his grip.

"As I thought." Ni-Ka-Re took it back, dandled it easily in one hand. "Since my friend Ahmose has vouched for you, young fellow, I had thought to apprentice you to a trimmer. But you will have to sharpen knives until you can wield one properly. And you will need more strength even for that. For now, you will help Dhuti cart away the offal." Ni-Ka-Re turned back to the lamb, severed its legs, and added its feet to the basket.

Imhotep felt rooted into the ground. *As if the work were not brutal enough, I will arrive home as dirty and malodorous as Dhuti, who looks as if he hasn't bathed in days.* But his filthy condition seemed not to bother Dhuti at all. He grinned up at Imhotep, until Ni-Ka-Re flicked his whip. A rosy welt joined the darker ones on Dhuti's shoulder.

Dhuti grabbed the basket by both handles and threaded his way past the tables where other blood-splashed apprentices labored. Toward the rear of the compound, out of Ni-Ka-Re's sight, Dhuti gestured toward a small, fenced area. "Watch Unas."

A huge, thick-necked man in a brief loincloth, caked stiff with dried blood, stood with a long, wicked-looking copper knife while two brawny boys brought in a cow, woven ropes tied tightly around its neck. Several shallow vessels sat on the ground behind the butcher. The beast seemed to be half-strangled already. One of the boys tied a rope to one of the cow's legs and pulled it up. The youths wrestled the animal to the earth. Imhotep felt the ground, along with his own innards, tremble at the impact.

Unas nodded, and one of the boys tilted the animal's head up while the other picked up one of the vessels. The cow's eyes rolled wildly, but before it could struggle out of position the butcher drew his knife across its throat in a quick, practiced motion. Imhotep sucked in his breath as the beast's blood gushed out into the bowl.

"They'll make puddings out of that," Dhuti said. Imhotep nodded. He'd often enjoyed Wabet's blood puddings at home.

The bigger of the two boys now grabbed one of the slaughtered cow's forelegs and began pumping it back and forth. Imhotep frowned. "What's he doing?"

"You have to get the blood out so that the meat doesn't spoil. That helps it drain faster."

"Ohhhhh. Interesting!"

Dhuti shrugged. "Perhaps. It's work, is what it is, I can tell you. If this cow were meant for a sacrifice or for the king's table, there'd be a priest here to inspect the blood and innards to make sure they are acceptable. But this beast is going to feed festival-goers, so that isn't necessary. Even so, of course, one must be careful."

The butcher now picked up a heavy stone-headed hammer. He took a practice swing or two. Then he drew the hammer back and swung it with all his strength, slamming it into the dead cow's skull with a sickening thud that made Imhotep wince. The man swung again, smashing the skull so that the brains spilled out.

Dhuti chortled. "Brains for supper!" He rubbed his stomach. "Most of it is for sale, but we'll get some as part of our wages."

He led Imhotep back to the gate where he once again dumped the contents of his basket into a woven-reed container twice the size of the ones by the butcher tables. Dhuti wrestled the large basket onto a sledge. "Now we feed the fish." Again, that foolish grin as he took up the ropes, handing one to Imhotep.

They pulled the sledge out of the compound and along the Street of White Walls until they reached the marketplace and then turned onto a well-worn path to the Nile. Soon Dhuti paused to urinate, braying like a donkey as he relieved himself.

Imhotep closed his eyes. Not from modesty but from sheer incredulity at being subject to a workplace composed of piss and excrement, dung and salt and offal. *How in the name of the Seven Hathors have I ended up here? It makes no sense! O my father, could you not have been more careful with your finances?*

All morning he trudged alongside Dhuti, carting away the waste as soon as the baskets were filled. There were hooves and ears, tails and snouts among the viscera. Flesh and bone turned to leather and stone; at least that's how they felt when he touched a rigid tail or a stiff ear. He examined a pig's nose, so similar to a man's. *How quickly the properties change. What does that signify for healing?*

Whap. Ni-Ka-Re's eyes bored into his. Imhotep's humiliation stung even more than the thin red line surfacing on his wrist. With a quick glance around, he noted Tesh-Pa's leer and the cool appraisal of a long-faced boy, a trimmer named Snefru. Imhotep snatched up the trimmer's basket for good measure and strode to the refuse area at the gate. These two baskets topped off the big container. Not waiting for Dhuti, he wrangled it onto the sledge, took up both ropes, and started for the river. He was three-quarters there by the time Dhuti caught up. "Never let Ni-Ka-Re catch you idle. Otherwise, the lash. But as soon as we get to the river, we can steal a few moments' rest."

By the water, Imhotep foraged some willow leaves, tore them into a neat pile, then spat on them, making a paste. Murmuring an incantation, he smeared it first on Dhuti's newest welt, then his own.

Dhuti's eyes went wide. "The sting is gone! How did you do that? Is it magic?"

"If I had more time, I could make something even better, but this will serve for now. I will show you how to make the poultice for yourself, but you must be careful to choose the right plant. The wrong one will have the opposite effect. And the spell is a simple one, easy to memorize."

Dhuti shook his head. "I cannot tell one plant from another. Besides, I am used to pain. And," he added, showing his gap-toothed grin, "you will be working alongside me."

Imhotep prayed that neither prediction would prove accurate.

∾

Long before the noon break Imhotep's stomach begged for food. His arms and back ached. How was he going to keep going even for the rest of this day?

At last, the other apprentices dropped their tools and sat under an acacia tree, devouring their provisions and talking amongst themselves.

Imhotep searched for the linen sack Wabet had prepared for him but it was no longer in the wooden box where he had left it. "Has anyone seen my meal?"

They stared blankly at him. One or two snickered.

"Describe it," said Tesh-Pa.

"Onions and dates and part of a loaf of bread in a linen bag."

Tesh-Pa shrugged. "Same as everyone else's."

"Someone has taken it."

The boy eyed him coldly. "Prove it, pig snout."

"I am called Imhotep."

"Not by me. I'll call you snout."

"And I'll call you jackass."

Tesh-Pa was on his feet in a flash.

"Ni-Ka-Re comes," hissed the long-faced boy.

Tesh-Pa backed off. But Ni-Ka-Re did not appear. "You are not wise to trick me, Snefru." Tesh-Pa rounded on the boy.

"I didn't, I wasn't—" Snefru squinted his close-set eyes. "Look!"

Ni-Ka-Re appeared, to Imhotep's surprise, and, judging by the expression on his face, to Snefru's as well. *A well-timed coincidence,* Imhotep said to himself.

"This way, Honored One." Ni-Ka-Re escorted a solemn-faced priest dressed in the sacred robes of Ptah into the shade. "You," he prodded Tesh-Pa with the whip, "fetch his Excellency a chair. Dhuti, get him a mug of beer."

The apprentices gaped, dumbstruck by the high-ranking visitor.

"Layabouts!" Ni-Ka-Re roared, whip at the ready. "Do you not hear me?" He kicked someone's lunch aside.

Imhotep managed to snatch a bit of bread in the rush to escape Ni-Ka-Re's wrath and gobbled it down.

"Is Ptah's priest often here?" he whispered to Snefru when he collected his basket of trimmings.

"Nay," the boy murmured. "Never before. Usually it's some lower-level holy man."

"What do you make of it?"

Snefru paused while cutting through a tendon. "Perhaps there will be a royal birth, and he is inspecting the meat in advance of a feast. Who knows?" With a few strokes of his blade, Snefru precisely trimmed the leg of lamb. "He will find none better, I assure you."

"And you have been here how long?"

Snefru narrowed his eyes. "What concern is that of yours?"

"I...only meant that you seem so proficient."

"Oh, well. Three years."

"Snout!" Tesh-Pa bellowed. "My basket overflows!"

Imhotep hurried over to fetch it before Tesh-Pa could yell that vile nickname a second time. He lugged his burden back to the gate. *Three years, Snefru said. But have there not been other feasts in all that time? And this is the first time he's seen this priest? I suppose he could have missed such a visitation, but I doubt it. Consider how we all gawked. Why the—*

Whap. The lash again. This time Imhotep's eyes watered as he slunk back to the gate. He busied himself piling all the soiled, stinking baskets on the sledge along with the last container of "fish food."

After the final long haul to the river, too weary to respond to Dhuti's chatter, Imhotep's work was finally, mercifully over. Filthy, exhausted, and ravenously hungry, he queued up at the gate for his wages, a small amount of grain and dates wrapped in a palm leaf. He took the leaf and turned to go, then tripped over an outstretched foot. The grain and dates went flying. He gathered them together as best he could while ignoring the laughter of the other apprentices.

Tired as he was, Imhotep welcomed the long walk home. He needed to shake off the stink and humiliation of the day, to hold it apart from his other, *real* life.

He detoured along the riverbank to wash off the blood and grime. Then he ferreted out a clump of lavender and uprooted a dozen spikes. If Wabet could spare the oil, he would prepare an ointment to mask the foul odor of the abattoir. For now, his ablutions at the Nile would have to suffice.

"Luck, luck, luck." Wabet blessed him as soon as he entered the house. "We have delayed the evening meal for you."

He had thought to decline but now he was too ravenous to refuse. Besides, the table bore roasted duck, two loaves of braided *ta* bread, a bowl of lentils, and a jar of wine.

He raised his brows.

"From Ahmose." Sebhot spread open his arms. "He is generous. Sit, Tep, so we can start."

He sat with his hands under the table to hide the lash on his wrist, but Kherry spotted the one on his shoulder.

"A clumsy fall." Imhotep shrugged, showing her his wrist, since she would notice it anyway. "An accident."

"I beg you be careful, my son." Her eyes filled. "I could not bear another loss to my family."

"Worry not, Mother. All is well." He would have to avoid the whip at any cost or, failing that, devise a way to conceal its marks.

After the meal, he sought his pallet on the roof, lowering himself onto it with a groan of relief. He locked his hands behind his head, gazing up at the stars. Some said that the stars were holes in Nut's cloak of night through which daylight shone. Others claimed that the stars were sparkling gems on Nut's body. But although most of them stayed in place, others moved slowly across the sky, changing position from night to night. Occasionally, though, one came loose, falling in a long streak of silent green light. Holes certainly could not fall from a cloak. Imhotep did not think that they were gems, but he could not be sure because none of the fallen ones had ever been found. But if they were not gems or holes, what were they? And what could cause them to move or fall?

He thought again of the entrails and severed limbs he had seen throughout the day. All animals had guts and legs, according to their kind.

Everything has a pattern, does it not? One only has to learn where to look. The rivers of blood in our bodies, the knots of veins, the sacs and bones, all have their own mysteries, their own immutable laws. I would give much to understand them!

He heard Sebhot's steps on the stairs. "How did you pass your day?" Imhotep asked.

"I went through Father's ledgers again."

"And did you find anything, brother?"

"No, no, no, and no," said Sebhot, as he settled on his pallet and unfastened his sandals. "There are no mistakes in the figures."

"Well, *something* is going on." Imhotep blew out his breath. "Perhaps we will go through them again, together," he said. "*Something* is wrong somewhere, and we will discover it." He turned over. "Tomorrow."

He tried to think about the ledgers, and the profits missing from their basement, but the numbers in his thoughts flew apart like birds fleeing a hawk. Too tired to think about anything except how weary he was, within moments he fell asleep.

7

Imhotep's second day at the abattoir was somewhat better than the first, because of his budding friendships with Snefru and Dhuti. Still seeking where best to employ his new apprentice, on this day Ni-Ka-Re put him to work with the salting crew. *Come,* thought Imhotep, *this is a relief!* Any task that took him even a short distance from the dripping trestles was to be appreciated, and he breathed a prayer of thanks to Thoth for assisting him.

Salting the mutton involved burying pieces of butchered sheep in natron, salt collected from dry lake beds. Most of it came from Wadi Natrun, a dry watercourse northwest of the city. Imhotep knew that the substance was used by embalmers like Merisu to preserve the dead and aid in their mummification. It also worked well to clean teeth and, as Hau had taught him, could be combined with other ingredients to treat wounds.

"It stings mightily, I know," Hau said, demonstrating natron's properties to Imhotep one day when Imhotep showed up with a cut sustained from an encounter with the knife-edged grass growing near the river. "But I tell you, injuries treated with natron tend to fester far less often than those remaining untreated. Why this should be, we do not know."

Imhotep, working with the meats, now thought he understood why: with less moisture in a wound, there was less to attract hungry maggots, giving injured flesh more of a chance to heal. In any case, the salt drew out moisture from the mutton and preserved it longer. He looked forward to discussing this insight with Hau.

During the course of the day, he lugged many baskets of meat to the salt pits, an area marked off from the rest of the grounds by a low mud-brick wall. The holes of varying sizes had been dug there to accommodate cuts of meat from sheep, cows, and game birds, then filled with natron. Meat buried in the salt pits dried out quickly as the moisture in it was absorbed. Selecting an empty pit, Imhotep dumped a basket of salt into it and took his time arranging the pieces of the butchered sheep within, then covered them with yet more salt. The mutton would be dry and ready for use within two days. Possibly some sailing vessel would use the preserved meat during a long voyage.

Thinking of this brought Thuya to mind, and Imhotep sighed. Everything in his life seemed to have conspired to trap him here, stuffing pieces of meat into a salt pit. Of what use was his clever heart here? He should be on the river, seeking new lands, exploring them, learning their customs and ways…

The crack of Ni-Ka-Re's whip and a sharp sting of the lash across his shoulders roused him from his thoughts and he hurried back to the trestles for more joints of meat before the overseer could cut him a second time. Though tears welled in his eyes, and he longed to cry out, he bit his lip against the pain and made no sound, determined not to show weakness in front of the other workers.

Not long before the midday meal break Ni-Ka-Re ordered him to the garbage heap behind the abattoir to dump a basket of offal. Keeping a wary eye on the stray dogs that hung around the place, Imhotep flung the morsels toward them. "You remind me that it's time for my own lunch."

Famished, he made his way to where he had left his linen lunch sack, beneath a palm tree with those of the other workers. Before he reached his food, however, he saw Tesh-Pa step forward and seize it.

"That's *mine*," Imhotep said angrily.

Tesh-Pa simply laughed. "Not anymore. You should be more careful. I am hungry enough to eat two lunches today. I may be tomorrow, as well."

Imhotep, accustomed from an early age to being picked on because he was thin and weedy, didn't hesitate. He knew that the only way to hold his own was to stand up for himself. He pushed the other apprentice hard in the chest, so that he staggered back. Tesh-Pa dropped the lunch bag and stepped forward in a fighting stance. Imhotep quailed inwardly but there was nothing else he could do now. He closed first, bringing his left fist up in a quick jab, but Tesh-Pa was ready.

It was over within moments. Imhotep lay sprawled in the dirt with a sore jaw. Tesh-Pa stalked away, after first stamping hard on Imhotep's lunch. Imhotep ate the smashed food anyway, ignoring the laughter of the other apprentices.

When he returned to work, Dhuti edged over to him and muttered, "Stay away from Tesh-Pa. He's got the disposition of a scorpion."

"I wasn't looking for trouble in the first place," Imhotep said in protest.

"But *he* was. He always is. He enjoys brawling. Just do your best to avoid him."

Good advice. Distracted by anger, however, Imhotep did not move quickly enough at his afternoon tasks to satisfy Ni-Ka-Re and before long had earned two more cuts of the whip across his shoulders, which did not help his mood.

On his return home he found Wabet and his mother in a state of suppressed excitement. "Look here!" Wabet exclaimed, pulling Imhotep into the kitchen. "See?" Beside the small cooking stove lay two big fish and two ducks, both quite fresh.

Imhotep blinked at the bounty. "More gifts from Ahmose, I suppose," he said.

"No!" Kherry said. "A guttersnipe of a boy delivered them, wrapped in leaves, this afternoon. He would not say who sent them, only that it was a man he did not know."

His mouth watered. *Perplexing, but welcome.*

Sebhot came in shortly thereafter and shook his head in puzzlement at the anonymous gift. "The food comes at a good time for us, though," he said. "Apparently our mysterious benefactor doesn't wish to be known."

That evening after dining with his family, Imhotep sat without wincing as his mother dressed the wounds with a salve of his own devising. The cooling effects of the ointment had the added benefit of easing his tension as well. He was so tired that he nearly fell asleep on the stool while she worked.

Sebhot reclined on his bed across the roof. Several scrolls lay piled on the rooftop beside him.

"Seb, what are you—ouch, Mother!"

"Well, you should do this yourself if you find my touch too heavy for you," she said with dignity, and set the pot of unguent down beside him.

He took it up and did as she suggested. He rubbed some extra salve into his blistered hands. They would form calluses soon enough, but in the meantime, he'd simply have to endure the discomfort and bleeding. Looking again at Sebhot, Imhotep said, "What are you reading?"

Sebhot dropped one scroll and picked up another. "Father's ledgers."

"Why?" Imhotep could not stifle the huge yawn that came suddenly. "We know the story they tell. It is as sad as Isis's long search for Osiris after he was killed by Set."

"Aye, and yet..." Sebhot shook his head. "Something is amiss. I can find nothing definite, but there *is* something, I know it."

My hands are bloody, while his are stained merely with ink. Yet Imhotep didn't wish to berate his brother.

Sebhot scowled at the scroll in his hands. "He *said* he put profits back in, but there should be more to show, if that were true. But I think it is true, because I know the going rates for goods and service. So where is the missing money?"

"Sebhot, honored brother—occupy yourself with other concerns, please. Such as, who sent us the fish and ducks? In any case, things are as they are."

Sebhot scoffed. "You sound like Father! You said we'd go over the ledgers today, Tep, remember? If you are not willing, leave it to me." With a scowl he returned to his study of the scrolls.

Imhotep said nothing, but Sebhot's accusing words struck deep. *Have I indeed become like Father? In truth, that did not sound like me. I have always asked questions and sought answers. But of late my thinking has grown dull. It's this butcher work. It is beating the curiosity out of me.* He lay awake pondering the changes in himself, listening to Sebhot muttering to himself as he went through the ledger scrolls.

&

When Imhotep arrived at the abattoir the next morning, Ni-Ka-Re eyed him while tapping the whip in his hand. "Today I wish you to work with Hori. I want to see how you do cutting joints."

"As you wish." Imhotep, determined to avoid the quick flick of the overseer's lash, vowed to himself that he would excel at the task.

He watched closely as Hori, the second most experienced butcher after Unas, instructed him about the knives. A muscular man of twenty or so with a very large nose, Hori never used two words when one would do. "Every day sharpen knife on whetstone, keep sharp." He held the blade for Imhotep's inspection. "When dull, sharpen again. You try."

Imhotep took the tool and balanced it in his hand. Well used as it was, the blade was nevertheless shining and sharper than the knife-edged grass growing along the Nile's banks. Hori let him practice incisions on a sheep's leg, showing him how to cut into the joint easily and quickly rather than saw through it by force. "Seek the knuckles of bone, cut through," he said. By day's end Imhotep, a quick study, could swiftly dismember a sheep. Getting the proper cuts from the body itself was a different matter. Hori, Unas, and Ni-Ka-Re conferred out of his earshot as Imhotep wiped his hands clean with straw. The overseer stumped over to him and said, "I am told you did well. Continue with him tomorrow, learn the different cuts of meat."

It was as close to praise that Imhotep had received from Ni-Ka-Re. He returned home feeling better about his work.

❧

The next day he paid close attention to Hori while the butcher showed him the cuts of a lamb. There were many more than the ten main ones he already knew: neck, shoulder, rib, breast, foreshank, loin, sirloin, tenderloin, leg, and hind shank. When the brain, lungs, and so forth were included, there were nearly fifty, with the prime ones destined for the king's table and the lesser ones for workers and commoners.

Trimming the meat was difficult and required a lot of concentration to be sure he got the different cuts correct. The blood didn't bother him; he had helped Hau staunch wounds and set broken bones. Once, the old healer even allowed him to extract a woman's inflamed tooth.

The day passed quickly. Imhotep came to find the work fascinating, and from it he gained a better understanding of the mechanics of animals. His lack of squeamishness won him a few grudging words of appreciation from Ni-Ka-Re.

At home, Imhotep found his brother increasingly testy after more fruitless inspection of their father's business records. "The figures seem to add up, but it's like feeding grain to a duck and watching it get thinner instead of fatter. I do not understand." At last Sebhot agreed to put the matter aside for the time being.

"This is a wise choice," Imhotep told him. "In a few days we will both return to the study with fresh hearts."

The next day he arrived at work to find the apprentices buzzing with the news that there would be a killing for the royal family that day: a cow was to be prepared for a festival.

"That's why the priest was here the other day," Dhuti said, nodding in understanding. "He was ensuring that Ni-Ka-Re was prepared for this task, with sanctified implements."

The actual slaughter did not occur until nearly noon, when the temple priest who had earlier visited the abattoir arrived to supervise. Ni-Ka-Re told the apprentices to bring the animal in from the holding pen behind the mud-brick building in which he had his small office.

It took the combined strength of all to lead the reluctant beast to the killing area. "She smells the blood," Ni-Ka-Re said, wiping the sweat off his forehead with the back of his wrist. "Knows what's in store for her."

Imhotep had grown used to the killings and no longer found their sheer violence as shocking as he had at first. He'd eaten meat numerous times at home because the family until recently had been well off. But before coming to the abattoir he'd never seen the beginning of the process: the killing of the creature and its subsequent butchering.

Because this was for a royal feast for King Sanakhe's table, the temple priest stood by to make sure all went according to prescribed ritual. He watched soberly as Ni-Ka-Re and the others donned the high-sole leather shoes they used to keep their feet out of the blood that would soon cover the ground. Ni-Ka-Re tied a rope to one of the cow's legs, then passed it over the animal's back and pulled it up tight. Off balance now on three legs, the cow could be pushed over with relative ease. The cow lowed in apprehension as its other legs were tied together.

As the priest intoned a spell, Ni-Ka-Re signaled Tesh-Pa and Snefru, the two biggest boys, to pull the cow's head back. The beast's dark wet eyes rolled in terror. Imhotep took up his position in front of the animal. This was not a preferred place, for whoever stood there was likely to be splashed by the first gush of the cow's blood. But as the newest addition to the workers, it was his duty.

The old priest intoned, "You are only an animal, but you die for a noble purpose, to become food. It is just, it is right. Be at peace." Imhotep raised a shallow pottery bowl, one of several by his side, placed there to catch the blood that would be used later in sacrificial rites, the cow having been blessed.

With one quick slice of his copper knife, Ni-Ka-Re cut the beast's throat. The jet of blood caught Imhotep full in the chest, but he was expecting it and did not flinch. The bowl quickly filled, as did four more before the flow slowed. The priest stepped forward and sprinkled sacred water on the gaping wound in the cow's throat.

Now it was time to cut the animal up into pieces. The apprentices, after arming themselves with hatchets, cleavers, knives, and saws, set to work under Hori's direction and the watchful eyes of the priest. Working swiftly, they cut off the legs and head. Tesh-Pa expertly skinned the cow and the others divided up the carcass. Imhotep himself carved the hind legs into three parts: thigh, knee-joint, and foot.

Ni-Ka-Re and the priest of Ptah inspected the carcass and judged the quality of the meat. The priest graciously accepted Ni-Ka-Re's gift of the spleen and the liver.

After the holy man's departure, Ni-Ka-Re took Imhotep aside. "You do well as a butcher, it seems," he said. "From now on you work with Hori."

Imhotep inclined his head. "I thank you, master," he said.

At day's end both Snefru and Dhuti congratulated him as they walked out into the street.

"I have been here two years with barely an increase in my situation," Dhuti said. "I don't know whether to be envious of you or happy for your good fortune."

"Chopping up animals is nothing to be envious about," said Imhotep, "and I don't feel particularly fortunate, though I suppose it's good that my wages will improve a little."

"You have a guarantee of future employment," said Snefru. "How could you not be pleased by that?"

"I do thank the gods for it," Imhotep replied, thinking of his family. "Yet it is not what my heart wishes for me."

"You are an odd person," said Dhuti with a grin. "And here we leave this intriguing discussion." He and Snefru turned down an alleyway toward their homes while Imhotep continued on his way.

He decided to take a detour to Rudjet's bakery in the hope of seeing the lovely Meresankh, but first he stopped at the river to wash off as much of the slaughtered cow's dried blood as he could, keeping a wary eye out for crocodiles as he did so. To his disappointment, Meresankh was not at work. Rudjet, usually a cheerful man, seemed distracted and careworn. Sensing trouble, Imhotep said, "Is all well, master?"

"Alas, it is my daughter," said the baker, frowning. "The clumsy thing burned herself this morning, and I fear she will not be able to do her work for at least a week."

Bouncing on his toes, Imhotep said, "Sir, I can make a poultice for her that will ease her pain and speed her healing." He knew he sounded eager but did not care.

The baker eyed him. Imhotep realized how he must look— wet, disheveled, his loincloth stained with blood he hadn't been able to rinse out of it. Plus, even after a quick wash in the Nile, he knew he smelled more like a sheep or a cow than a man. But all Rudjet said was, "She has been seen by the healer Thethi. He rubbed ointment on her burned arm, but it seems to have had little effect."

"Old Thethi! I know of him," said Imhotep, unable to keep the scorn out of his voice. "His knowledge is…" He paused, licking his lips. It was not wise to denigrate his elders. "A poultice would serve Meresankh better than a salve," he went on. "A burn needs air. Or so I have been taught by Hau."

"Hau the healer? He is your teacher? He sometimes buys bread from me," said Rudjet. "He is well regarded. Hmmm. Very well, young master, if you can alleviate my daughter's suffering and get her back to work, I would be grateful."

"I will have something for her tomorrow morning."

Imhotep hurried off, feeling an expansion of joy in his chest that wiped away his weariness. He would gladly roll in the mud if it would impress Meresankh, but relieving her pain was even better.

8

At home he learned that they had received another mysterious gift of food: three big fish and a duck. As before, there was no hint of who had sent the provisions. He changed his loincloth and scraped off the day's remaining blood as best he could, gobbled his dinner, and then rummaged through his box of herbs and charms, searching for the makings of a good healing poultice. He had most of what he needed except almond oil, which was light enough to be quickly absorbed by the skin.

Hau will have some almond oil, he thought. It would be wise, as well, to make sure that his poultice would be effective, and even though he trusted his judgment it was a good idea to have Hau look it over. Plus, Hau was better at healing spells.

Despite the lateness of the hour—the sun was setting, and no prudent person liked being out past dark—Imhotep was too impatient to wait until the morning. He trotted to Hau's home on the outskirts of Mennefer near the river. The old man was sitting in front of his small mud-brick dwelling, letting the last rays of the sun bathe him.

Most days Hau gave lessons in healing magic at the work area beside his home. It was little more than a lean-to of reeds, beneath which was a crude table littered with small jars of stone and ceramic along with some old scrolls.

"Who comes? Who comes?" he asked, startling at Imhotep's approach. "Who—oh, it is you." He settled back on his bench. "What is it you are after?"

"Why must I be 'after' something, master?" Imhotep asked, squatting on the ground beside Hau. "Could I not be here simply to visit?"

Hau chuckled. "Visit? You are one of the least sociable

people I know, spending all your time memorizing incantations and collecting herbs and studying animals and watching the stars." He chuckled again. "I sometimes think that if every person in the world were to disappear, you would not notice until you needed something to eat."

"That's not fair. I have friends."

"Eh, eh. You have family and associates."

Imhotep frowned. "But I *do* have friends, and one has been burned. I wish to make an effective poultice to reduce her pain."

"Oh, *her* pain, is it? Eh, eh!"

Imhotep felt his face flush but drew himself up. "I need some almond oil. Do you have any?"

"Almond oil? Yes, but tell me the rest of the ingredients, and tell me what spells you will chant." He listened closely as Imhotep listed the items in the recipe and described the spells. Hau then said, "You have chosen well, though your spell does not invoke Heka."

Imhotep blinked at him. "But Heka is present in all."

Hau waved this objection away. "Yet you call on Ma'at. Why?"

"For...harmony and balance. Meresankh's life is disturbed because of her injury. Is it not proper to bring her back into balance?"

"Certainly, but Heka it is who *makes* balance, harmony, and every other concept or aspect of life possible! He is like the air we breathe but cannot see, he is everywhere, endless and eternal. Do you not remember my teachings?" He shook his head in mock despair.

Imhotep, spotting the twinkle in the old man's eyes, restrained a grin. "I remember. You taught me that Heka says, 'To me belonged the universe before you gods came into being. You have come afterwards because I am Heka.'"

"Mmm. And what number spell do those lines come from?"

"Number 261, master."

"Ah, *now* he remembers. Yes. Now adjust your spell accordingly, Imhotep, and your friend will recover quickly."

Darkness thickened around the city. Imhotep ran home, cursing himself for not having brought an oil lamp or at least a torch, even though it was still only the early evening; ghosts would not begin their nightly search for life until later.

He arrived at home out of breath but unscathed. Before retiring for the night, he mixed the potion for the poultice and wrote out a new spell.

❧

He woke early the next day and was standing outside Rudjet's bakery stall when the man appeared, ready to light the fires under the ovens. Taking the poultice from his carrying bag, Imhotep said, "I can apply this very quickly, master, and speak the spell. But I must hurry lest I be late for work."

"Mmm." Rudjet eyed the small pot of unguent and sniffed at it. "In truth it has a more pleasing scent than the one Thethi used."

"I verified this mixture with Hau himself." Imhotep shifted his weight from one foot to the other while Rudjet, never a hasty man, pondered.

At last, the baker said, "Come through, then, and I will call Meresankh."

Like most craftsmen and tradesmen, Rudjet lived in the building directly behind his stall. Imhotep followed him into a small courtyard, where Meresankh sat beside a persimmon tree. She was pale but her arm was an angry red in color. Imhotep felt his heart quail at the sight of her burn, which was relatively severe, but he quickly got hold of himself as she turned her weary eyes to him and smiled.

"Tep," she said. "What a nice surprise."

Imhotep heard the pain in her voice but could not help grinning foolishly. Her father said, "He is not visiting, he has a poultice for your arm. Imhotep, proceed."

Without a word, but smiling at Meresankh, Imhotep knelt by her side. Spreading a clean linen bandage gently across the burn, he slowly poured the unguent over it and then wrapped the clean length loosely around her arm. This was the first time he had ever touched the girl. Her skin was soft and smooth, and she smelled faintly of sage. A pleasing, excited flutter tickled his midsection. He took a few leaves from his linen bag. "Chew one of these this morning, and one this afternoon. They will help with the pain. I—I will stop by after my work," he said. "I believe that by then you will see an improvement."

He would gladly have stayed to talk with her, but he knew that if he was late, he'd feel Ni-Ka-Re's lash. He therefore bid farewell to Meresankh and hurried on his way, after accepting a small bun from a grateful Rudjet. He devoured it as he trotted along Mennefer's crowded streets, brushing crumbs from his chest as he arrived at the abattoir.

The day passed much more slowly than usual, or so it seemed to Imhotep as he labored, wielding his knife under Hori's watchful eyes. Upon the completion of the workday, he all but flew down the street, dodging passersby and once tripping over a cat that darted out of an alleyway. He nearly hurled an imprecation after the animal but caught himself at the last moment before the words passed his lips. Nevertheless, he sent a fervent prayer to Bast to apologize for thinking ill of one of her people.

Rudjet was not in his stall, and the baked goods had been withdrawn for the night. Imhotep rapped on the reed doorway that acted as a barrier between the stall and the modest home behind it. A woman, small and pretty but with gray rings beneath her eyes, answered his knock. Her resemblance to Meresankh was striking.

"I am Imhotep," he said, bowing. "I gave your daughter a poultice for her burn this morning and I wanted to ask after her health."

The woman smiled. "I am her mother, Betrest," she said. "I thank you, for she is much improved. Whatever was in your poultice has relieved her pain and the redness is going away. But she is sleeping now, Imhotep. I pray you look in tomorrow morning and she will be awake."

"I will," he said, "and I will renew the poultice then as well."
Betrest picked up a basket of bread that sat in a corner. "A
gift for your healing skills," she said.

He went on his way with a sprightly step and joy in his heart.
For the next three days he looked in on Meresankh and
changed her dressing. It was no great hardship. On each day,
Betrest gave him bread. By the end of the third day Meresankh
was much improved.

"I will go back to work in Father's bakery tomorrow," she
said, smiling at him. "Imhotep, you are an amazing person!"

He blushed, but this time he enjoyed the flushed warmth of
his cheeks. "I was confident that my methods would be better
for you than…than those of anyone else."

She laid her hand on his arm. "And so they have been. You
should come to visit me, even if you don't have a poultice for
me. I would have us be friends."

"Thank you, I would like that." He departed, aware of the
foolish grin on his face but not caring.

The days fell into a steady rhythm. Imhotep left his home early
in the morning, worked all day, collected an occasional lash
mark, drew his wages, and fell into bed each evening, praying
for a sign from Thoth that somehow this miserable time would
pass.

Meanwhile, the atelier's business continued to suffer in the
wake of Kaneferw's death. Lord Horemheb decided to withdraw his commission, which had been for the design and construction of his tomb; a sizable sum was thereby lost. The only
bright light in Imhotep's existence was his growing friendship
with Meresankh, which was as delicious and nourishing to him
as his mother's lentil stew.

At irregular intervals another packet of food would myste-
riously appear by the front door. There was never a hint about
who the family's unknown benefactor might be.

"You know your slave friend, Odji," said Sebhot one evening. "He has come by more than once looking for lessons, but you've been asleep."

"Oh, I had forgotten him," said Imhotep guiltily. "He is an apt student."

Sebhot nodded. "He is, and I have shown him a few things. But the next time he comes I think you should resume your teachings."

"I will, I promise."

He clasped his hands behind his head. So many responsibilities! He missed Kaneferw more than ever, understanding now how well his father had kept the family afloat. Imhotep was pleased that his wages were holding the family together, even though their circumstances were reduced. All would be better if only Kherry could be roused from her misery. She had grown increasingly sad following his father's death. Though he occasionally visited Meresankh, Imhotep spent as much time as he could with his mother, seeking a way to lighten her heart.

One day around sunset, after his butchering work, he sat in front of Hau, pondering his mother's condition while the old man droned on about proper spell-casting. Hau rapped on the table with his walking stick. "You are not paying attention to my words!"

"Your pardon, master," said Imhotep.

"What ails you, boy?"

Imhotep took no offense at the old man's choice of words. Hau habitually called everyone younger than him *boy*. "Don't be cross," Imhotep said. "It is Mother. She becomes more morose and distant each day. She sleeps poorly and is listless when awake. She half-hears what is said to her and speaks little. She grows thin. I fear a demon has entered her."

Hau rubbed his whiskery chin. "Possible, possible. The blasted things do love a mournful person. What would you want, Imhotep?"

"I would have my mother back as she was," said Imhotep, staring at his feet.

"Hmpf, of course, of course." Hau grabbed a scroll and unrolled it. "Ah yes. A potion against melancholy. It will eject the demons from your mother's body." He cast a sharp glance at Imhotep. "It requires crocodile dung, which I lack." He let go of the scroll and it rolled back up with a snap. "Come—we will go to the river at once."

Soon they were making their way gingerly along a section of the riverbank, looking for crocodile droppings.

"They are sly beasts," Imhotep said.

Hau scoffed. "The gods send us challenges each day." He squinted at the ground. Hau's sight might have grown less acute with the passage of time, but his other senses were undiminished. He sniffed the air. "Aha! Do I smell what I think I smell?" With his walking staff, Hau waved happily at the river below the bank.

A few arms' lengths down the bank the Nile lay sluggish and dark. At its very edge Imhotep saw a splatter of semi-liquid waste. "So it would seem," he said. "It's too small for a hippo, and does not have the aspect of that animal's leavings."

"Excellent! I think we are in luck."

While Hau waited, Imhotep slid down the bank. Close to the mess, he wrinkled his nose. "Phew! A crocodile for sure." He swiftly gathered up the reeking pile in two large leaves, then wrapped them with a length of vine. He scrambled up the bank away from the river and reached up to grasp the old man's staff, which Hau held out to assist him.

Back in Hau's workroom, Imhotep watched with interest as his teacher combined the stinking crocodile feces with other substances to produce a few handfuls of evil-looking and worse-smelling ointment.

It's a pity he can't devise something with a scent as pleasing as Meresankh's poultice, Imhotep thought. *Mother won't like this. I will make it my business, when I am creating potions and such, to be sure they are carefully perfumed and pleasing to the nose...that way people will be more willing to use them.*

After speaking a few spells over the stuff, Hau said, "This is some of the best I've ever made." He smeared a portion of it into a small stone jar and handed it to Imhotep. "For your mother," he said, showing the gaps in his teeth with a wide grin.

"Thank you, teacher." Imhotep accepted the foul-smelling trophy. "I'll have to keep it outside in the back, though. She won't allow this in the house."

"Eh, eh…when she is rid of her demons, she will be of a different heart. Have her spread this on her arms and chest twice a day."

"I will tell her. I hope she will agree."

9

As he had feared, however, Kherry proved most reluctant to use the pungent concoction.

"Faugh!" she cried upon smelling it. "Another of Hau's atrocities? By the gods! Each one smells worse than the last. How does he do it?"

"Please, Mother," Imhotep said. "You have been so sad and unhappy of late. I fear the working of a malignant spirit. Hau and I only wish to help you. Try it for a few days and see what difference it makes."

She sighed deeply. "Very well, my son. I know it has been a difficult time. I will try to follow the instructions. But can't he make *any*thing that doesn't smell like...well, *you* know."

She would use only a small amount and flatly refused to wear it during the day. "It's bad enough I must smell myself...I'm not having everyone else I meet sniffing me as though I were a dog that has been rolling in offal." And Imhotep had to be satisfied with that.

After Kherry applied the stuff to her skin, Imhotep took the jar out into the rear courtyard, where he had built a small mud-brick enclosure as a workshop. He placed the little pot on a rack made from dried reeds and blessed it with a few suitable spells to keep flies away. He molded a leaf around the mouth of the jar and secured it with twine.

He started at the sound of someone clearing his throat.

He turned and saw Odji. The boy bowed his head. "Hullo," Imhotep said. "Sebhot told me you'd been around. I apologize for not being available for our lessons."

"That's all right. I know you have been distracted by your father's death."

Imhotep took a piece of pottery from the pile in the basket by the doorway. He opened his scribe's palette and handed

Odji's to him. The slave didn't dare keep one in his quarters for fear Ahmose would find it. "We were on determinatives, I believe?"

Odji poured a few drops of water onto the cake of ink in his palette and screwed up his face in a comical way. "Let me think..."

Imhotep smiled. Odji couldn't resist fooling around, but his memory was excellent, and he was an eager student.

"Ah, I remember. Classes of objects." Odji darted a glance at Imhotep, who nodded. "We never need them when speaking aloud, but when we write, we must have them."

"Good! Now an example."

Odji took his stylus, wiped it on the wet ink cake, and wrote *scribe* using the symbol *sesh*. "Correct?" Imhotep nodded. Odji added another stroke above the symbol. "Now it means 'write.'"

"Excellent! Before long you'll be able to work for Chancellor Pepi himself."

Odji's face darkened. "I would not work for that old jackal even if it meant my life." He bit at a knuckle. "Your pardon. I know he is a friend of your family."

Imhotep lifted a dismissive hand. He knew that Odji's sister, Noha, was one of Pepi's slaves. The two were from Kush and had been captured in a raiding party when young. Their parents were killed, and the two children were put on the block to be sold. Ahmose bought Odji, and Pepi purchased Noha.

"Pepi is not a harsh master," Odji said, "but he takes advantage of her in...in other ways."

"I have heard such, of his female slaves." Imhotep remembered what Pepi himself had said to him not long before: "Our parents are not always the people we think they are." *Apparently that truth also extends to other people, such as family friends.* "It is regrettable."

Odji shrugged. "It is the same everywhere. In Kush there were slaves, and we thought of them as little more than furniture, or perhaps trained animals. Why should it be different here? Ahmose at least does not beat me. But he would not like it if he knew I was learning what a scribe knows. He thinks Kushites should be kept in their place."

By the time the lesson was done twilight was far advanced, and the stars were peeping out. Odji promised to practice his brushwork, then waved farewell and ran out into the street. Imhotep watched him go. He knew that the Kushite boy shrugged off the possibility of wandering ghosts. "It is not far to Ahmose's residence," he had said after their first lesson, weeks ago, "and I am very fleet of foot." Still, Imhotep thought Odji brave for defying the spirits and sent a prayer of safekeeping after him.

Feeling hungry, Imhotep went inside to see if there were any dates. He found his mother sitting on the floor in front of the altar, weeping. Wabet looked at Imhotep, her own eyes sad. She stood and went to a corner. Imhotep followed her, and they spoke in low voices so as not to disturb Kherry.

"She is not well." Wabet twisted a lock of her hair as she always did when distraught.

"I see that," Imhotep said. *Hau's crocodile-dung salve is not working.* "I wish I knew what I could do to help her." He crossed the room and knelt by Kherry's side.

"Mother."

"Oh, Imhotep. I miss him so."

"We all do, Mother."

She shook her head. "Now I will not see him until I cross to the Beautiful West. I feel so tired, so dull, as if all the color has drained from the world. How can I bear to go on living?" A tear trickled down her cheek. "Perhaps I, too, should go to the West now, to be with him. In truth I do not wish to be here."

With a chill he took in the meaning of her words. Cradling her head in his hands, he closed his eyes and addressed a prayer to Sekhmet, the lioness-headed goddess of healing. *Come, you who expel evil. Smash the demons plaguing my mother.* By the time he was done with the prayer, Sekhmet—or some other beneficent god, perhaps Thoth—had given him the answer.

There was a plant he knew of from his studies with Hau, a tall shrub with dark green leaves and red berries. He remembered the day Hau had told him about it. Holding up a sprig of the plant for Imhotep to inspect, Hau had said, "The ones who dwell in the desert, the nomads, they chew these berries when they are tired." He gave four to Imhotep, who popped them in his mouth, grimacing at the bitter taste.

But within a very short time he was possessed of strength and well-being and felt more energetic. Remembering that uplift in spirit, he smiled in the darkness. They'd be perfect to restore his mother's mood. There was one such plant in a walled garden belonging to the home of a nobleman not far away. He and Sebhot had climbed the wall more than once in search of sweet, tangy persimmons, and he remembered seeing one of the red-berry bushes there, probably used for decoration.

"Fear not, Mother," he said. "I pray you, use Hau's salve for another few days. I will write a new spell. I promise you that soon all will be well."

"I would love to believe you, my son," Kherry said, wiping away a tear. "I am so tired…I will sleep now."

"And I," he replied. He took his leave and went up to the roof, where Sebhot was already asleep. Although he was indeed weary from a long day of working and Odji's lesson, Imhotep lay down on his pallet and gave himself to thought. The wise thing to do would be to discuss the red-berry plant with Hau, but he was certain that its effects would help his mother.

He could not simply present himself at the nobleman's door; the man was ill-tempered and unfriendly to all. Nor could Imhotep gain entry to the garden during the day, for someone would see him climbing the wall and raise an alarm. The only way to obtain the berries was to steal them under cover of darkness. He didn't like the idea of thievery, for it might weigh against him on Ma'at's scales. His mother's welfare, however, was more important. His concern for her outweighed his fear of wandering ghosts.

Impatiently he watched the stars above as they slowly

progressed across the sky. Sebhot's regular breathing did not change. Imhotep stayed awake, waiting for the other members of the household to fall asleep. At last, he rose and stole downstairs, listening for signs of wakefulness. To his satisfaction, the deep breathing of Kherry and Wabet told him they were journeying through the country of dreams.

Beginning to perspire now that the time for action had come, he touched his amulet, praying that the spells he and Hau had created to ward off spirits would protect him, and slipped out the door into the darkness cloaking the Two Lands.

He slunk through the empty streets. Most people by now were fast asleep up on their rooftops. Despite his abiding fear of ghosts, he enjoyed being abroad on a secret errand. Within a short time, he was crouched beneath the nobleman's garden wall. Previously it had taken both him and Sebhot to scale it, but he was considerably taller than he'd been two years ago. He eyed the wall. *I can climb up there on my own.*

The noble had slaves, of course, but Imhotep had never seen any of them in the garden. Besides, no one would be expecting anyone to steal the red berries, which were kept primarily for their decorative value. He jumped, grabbed the top of the wall, and scrambled up. He scanned the garden below, and the dark house half hidden in foliage. All was quiet, nothing moved.

Suddenly he heard a snort from above. He froze, heart pounding. Those in the house were bedded down on its roof in the heat, as so many of Mennefer's inhabitants did. The snort came again, and a snore. Imhotep relaxed a little.

They sleep. There is nothing to fear.

He dropped lightly to the ground and moved at a half-crouch through the plants toward his target. From it he tore off a small branch laden with the berries, then hurried back to the wall, up and over it and down to the street. Excitement coursed through him as though he had eaten a handful of the berries. Now all he had to do was get back home unseen by man or spirit, and—

Voices stopped him in his tracks. At least two people, men (he assumed, though you couldn't always be sure with demons), were coming toward him in the street ahead. With a curse at his ill luck, he stepped into an alley, intending to wait until they passed. Sweat dripped down his torso.

The two men came nearer. From their stifled laughter and uncertain steps, Imhotep deduced they were drunk and stumbling home. The thought of ghosts obviously didn't trouble them.

Their words, at first obscure, became clearer as they drew closer to Imhotep's hiding place. One of the men said something Imhotep could not catch, but he did hear the other man say, "You worry too much."

His eyes went wide. *I know that voice!*

When the men came abreast of the alley, he shrank farther back into the shadows, willing himself to be still until they passed. Imhotep squinted. He made out the shape of two men, one small and slender, one thick and—*Ahmose!*

They paused at the mouth of the alley.

"Here, give me that flagon," Ahmose said.

"It is almost empty."

"Then it will be entirely empty when I finish."

Ahmose staggered into the alley, heading straight for Imhotep.

Imhotep's heart jolted in his chest. He looked around. The alley was not long, but there was a pile of debris at the far end. He jumped toward it, hearing Ahmose whistling tunelessly as he approached. Imhotep ducked behind the pile of rubble and shrank down just as Ahmose halted, swaying. Imhotep, fearing that he'd been spotted, instead heard Ahmose's whistling grow louder, and then heard liquid splashing.

He exhaled. *He is merely relieving himself.*

He risked peeking out from behind the trash and saw Ahmose using both hands as he finished urinating to tuck himself back into his loincloth, still whistling.

Then Ahmose used his supposedly injured hand to drain the flagon.

Imhotep's eyes narrowed. *Why—there's nothing wrong with his left arm at all, not even with his hand. He's perfectly fine. What in Thoth's name...?*

Ahmose left the alley. The voices died away. After a few moments, Imhotep extricated himself from the pile of trash. Skirting the puddle in the middle of the alley, he made his way back home. He crept up to the roof, placed the berry branch by his bed, and composed himself for sleep. But he tossed from side to side. Ahmose's arm was not injured, certainly not broken. Why then did he pretend it was?

And that other man's remark, "You worry too much." What was Ahmose worried about? Being discovered as a fraud? Clearly Ahmose, whom Imhotep had known as a trusted partner of his father, was not what he seemed. He was a liar for one, telling untruths about being injured, and was consorting with rough characters for another.

If Ahmose had lied about his arm, what else might he be lying about?

10

The next morning, before he left for work, Imhotep gave some of the red berries to his mother. At first reluctant, Kherry allowed herself to be persuaded to chew them. "Terrible," she said, making a face. "They taste the way Hau's potion smells. I hope they do not make me ill."

"I am sure they will not. I must go." He kissed her and left the house. Stopping briefly at Rudjet's bakery to inquire after Meresankh, he was delighted to see the girl at work, laying out fresh loaves. She broke into a wide smile at the sight of him.

"You are a great healer," she said. "My arm scarcely pains me at all now." She displayed it proudly. He saw that the skin was pink and healthy.

"I am so glad you are feeling better," he said, blushing. His own skin had improved in appearance as well, an unexpected benefit of his hard work and exercise, and he felt more confident talking to her than he once had.

"I want you to come to our evening meal today, or as soon as you can manage it," she said.

"Oh, uh, I would be most honored to accept." He frowned, thinking of his mother. He had to know how she was faring after eating the berries. "But tonight I cannot. I will come tomorrow, if the invitation stands."

"Of course."

Imhotep felt an absurd happiness as he sauntered through Mennefer's winding byways toward work. Empty of pedestrians last night—except for Ahmose and his mysterious associate—this morning they were full of movement and color, and everything seemed interesting.

Even his labors at the butcher shop seemed easier to bear. Thoughts of Meresankh distracted him so that the sting of Ni-

Ka-Re's whip across his shoulders shocked him. He cried out in surprise.

"Imhotep! Save your breath and your attention for your work," said the master butcher. "I'll have no daydreaming here!"

Imhotep bit back a sharp retort, knowing that any sort of back talk might get him flogged. A stroke or two of the whip was bad enough; a flogging would be far worse. He bent to his work without a word. Nearby, Tesh-Pa sniggered at him, touched his nose, and mouthed, *Snout!* Imhotep glared at him but said nothing. Raising his knife he sliced savagely through a sheep's haunch, imagining it to be Tesh-Pa's belly. The good mood with which he had begun his day evaporated like a puddle of water on hot stone.

After work, still simmering with anger from the punishment and the embarrassment of having yelped in pain, he made his way home. He was pleasantly surprised to see Kherry in the kitchen area, working with Wabet.

"Mother! You seem…better."

She said, "Do you know, I *feel* better, son. Such a clever one you are."

"So those berries helped stimulate you," he said. "I am so glad! I simply want you to be happy."

She sighed. "Happy? Well, that's another question. Still, I do feel better. I even went to the market today."

Pleased and relieved that the red berries had helped his mother, he couldn't wait to tell Hau about it. *It just proves that I shouldn't be slaving in a butcher shop; I should be learning and studying. I could do far more good for people as a healer than as a butcher.*

Lying on his pallet later than night, his thoughts turned again to Ahmose.

Why had he lied about his arm being broken? Imhotep knew he was by nature a trusting person, but now he could not help wondering what Ahmose was up to.

The following evening, he took a meal with Meresankh's family.

After dining he and Meresankh sat in the small open courtyard of her home, telling stories and joking. Imhotep enjoyed
the opportunity to spend time with her and found his heart
growing ever warmer as they chatted. "Your father greeted me
almost like an old friend," he said half-playfully to her.

She gave him an impish look. "Can you not guess why?"

"No, I can't. Please enlighten me."

"Truly you cannot guess?"

"I swear I cannot."

"Oh, Imhotep. I am of a marriageable age." She looked
away. "Your family…well, I think he seeks to make a match of
us."

Thunderstruck, he stared at her, mouth open. By Thoth, she
was right. He was thirteen, no older than Meresankh, and a
bit young for betrothal, but even so… "I would find that a
most…I mean, I would…uh." He heart pounded in his chest.
Would he marry Meresankh? He tried again to speak. "I would
be honored," he said.

"Is this a formal proposal?" she asked quietly, a smile on her
lips.

He blinked. "It may be! But hold. I have yet to deal with…"
He did not want to tell her how little money he had; clearly
her father hoped to gain prestige by having his daughter marry
into Imhotep's more well-to-do family. "Certain obligations,"
he finished lamely. "You know that I mean to take some time
off and journey to the south to study healing."

"Yes, and I know that your father's death has delayed that.
You have had to work in the abattoir."

"And your father…knowing that, he would still wish to ally
our houses?"

"My father may be only a baker, but he is no fool. He sees
your potential."

"He does me honor," said Imhotep.

"He saw how well your salve healed my burns," said the girl.

"I saw that too. My heart contains great love for you, Imhotep,"
she finished in a whisper.

Somehow a kiss seemed the inevitable response, and before he knew it, the thing had been done. And then one or two more.

"I never dared to wonder if you might become my wife. If we agree on it, and if you can wait until my return, I will be more experienced. And I may be able to go to work for myself, as healer."

"I will work with you in your shop," Meresankh said.

Imhotep laughed. "And what will your honorable father Rudjet do without you to assist him in *his* work?"

"Oh, he will hire someone. Do not have any concerns on that account."

"It shall be as you say," Imhotep replied, and took her in his arms again.

Days passed in an endless march of heat, blood, and the stench of meat going bad. Occasionally he would visit Meresankh, and never departed from her company without a feeling of elation. He spoke to Rudjet about marrying Meresankh, and found the baker was indeed agreeable to the prospect. Imhotep, tiring of thinking about the missing atelier profits, began to ponder the mysteries of married life. There was much he did not know about having a wife. He regretted the loss of his father, who could have guided him. The one best suited to do that now was Hau, but the old healer had never had a wife either, so Imhotep was reluctant to broach the subject.

For his family's sake Imhotep did his best to keep his mind on his work. He slept like a stone and ate like a hyena. When he managed to stay awake, he would watch the stars and note his observations in a scroll he kept by his bed. Occasionally he would imagine where his sailor friend Thuya was by now and feel a pang of regret that he could not be along for the adventure. Were the stars different in Nubia? Even his time with Hau was curtailed of necessity, because he was often too tired to go forage for herbs with the old man.

One morning he consulted his calendar as usual to see whether the day would be lucky or unlucky. The calendar, a slab of clay marked with the days of the months, was used year in and year out. It showed the year as consisting of three seasons of 120 days each. Each season was divided into four months of thirty days. He was pleased to see the day's religious prescription was favorable. "If you see anything on this day, it will be good," he muttered, reading the note on the other side of the calendar.

Of course! he thought. *That's because in three days it will be the Feast of the New Moon. Thoth is the God of the Feast; how then could this not be a good day for me?*

Later, at the butcher shop, Imhotep, filthy with his daily coating of sweat and blood, lugged a basket of meat and levered it into position beside other offerings on a long table set up in the courtyard. He suddenly realized that a month ago he couldn't have dragged that weight by himself, let alone hoist it above his waist. His boredom and unhappiness dissipated for a moment, and he addressed a quick prayer of thanks to Isis:

> *Goddess of Life,*
> *Beautiful in heaven,*
> *Heaven is in peace.*
> *Earth is in peace.*
> *All praise to You.*
> *I adore You, Lady Isis!*

The Feast of the New Moon gave the apprentices a two-day break from their labors. Imhotep took advantage of the holiday to do something he hardly ever did—nothing. He caught up on his sleep, visited Hau and other friends, and lazed around, surprising his family and even himself with his inaction while enjoying it thoroughly.

He chewed a date, pondering the recent turns his life had taken. *It's amazing how the things I normally find so fascinating—healing, magic, even the study of architecture—can be so easily ignored by people who have to work at a daily job; there simply isn't any time to do much else but work, and I usually have no extra energy to pursue other interests.*

On the day before Imhotep was scheduled to return to the abattoir, Odji came by. After his period of inactivity, Imhotep was pleased to do something that required some thought. And foremost in his thoughts these days was Ahmose. The man was, he knew, on site at an excavation, which allowed Odji to slip away for a writing lesson before Ahmose's return that evening.

"How is your master's arm?" Imhotep asked casually, moistening his ink cakes.

Odji snorted. "It doesn't seem to trouble him at all now. He says his healer has done wonders for him."

"I see." Odji knew nothing of medicine or spells and wouldn't understand how impossible it was for Ahmose's arm to be healed so quickly; but Imhotep knew. He had no time to ponder the news, however, for Odji dug into his loincloth for a small scrap of papyrus. He handed it to Imhotep, who examined it.

"A list of numbers? From a ledger? It looks like it's been burned."

"It has been. Ahmose was burning some old records. But that's not what I wanted to show you. Turn it over," said Odji.

"Oh." On the other side Odji had scrawled a symbol.

"What does this mean?"

"Hmm. It's not a sign I recognize," said Imhotep. "Where did you see it?"

"On the sole of Nekure's left foot."

"Nekure? Who is that?"

"A friend of Ahmose." Odji made a face.

Noticing Odji's sour expression, Imhotep said, "You don't like him, eh?"

"He is a rat. All of Ahmose's friends are rats, or louts, or both."

"This Nekure…is he small and thin?"

"Why, yes. How did you know?"

"Oh, I saw them together a few days ago. When did you see this mark on his foot?"

"He came yesterday, and I served them drinks. His sandals were off and his feet up, and I saw the mark. I thought it might be a birthmark, but it doesn't look like one."

"It's definitely not a birthmark. Why don't you like him?"

"For one thing, he only ever comes at night. Who does their visiting only at night? Only those who can't be trusted, *I* think. Plus, he calls me 'stupid Kushite' and throws date pits at me."

"Hmmm. May I take the papyrus to Hau and ask him?"

"Yes, of course, as long as you tell me what he says."

"I promise I will."

"Thank you. You know, Ahmose has something on *his* left foot too."

Imhotep cocked his head to one side. Even more interested now, he said, "Something on his foot? Do you have another scrap?"

"No, but I memorized its shape."

"Draw it for me. Please." He handed Odji a blank piece of pottery and an inked brush. The slave drew carefully on the shard. Imhotep stared at the symbol.

He shook his head. "I don't recognize this, either." Odji's shoulders slumped.

"Yet there is *something* about it…" Imhotep sucked in a deep breath. "I will take it to Hau. He is very wise. Odji, if you see any more markings like this, please let me know. It's all very curious."

"I better go now," Odji said. "It's late and Ahmose will be home soon." With that, he took his leave.

It was only after Odji left that it occurred to Imhotep that he should have asked him where the burnt scrap had come from. Financial records had been much in his mind of late, and he couldn't help but wonder what records Ahmose might have been destroying.

11

Imhotep customarily brought a small pot of unguent to work with him and applied it to his muscles when they troubled him. One day during the noon meal he sat under a palm tree in the abattoir's yard with the rest of the apprentices, rubbing the fragrant salve into his biceps. He saw Snefru watching him with obvious curiosity. Imhotep held the pot out to him. "Care to give it a try?"

Snefru eyed it. "You gave some of this stuff to Dhuti a while back."

"I did, and it eased his aches. This is an improved recipe. Go ahead, try it."

Snefru frowned. "Well, why not? Isis knows how stiff I get after a day lugging meat around." He slathered the stuff on his chest and arms. "It's…quite cool. I didn't expect it to feel that way."

"I put some mint into this batch. Keep it, Snefru; I have more at home."

"Many thanks, Imhotep."

Tesh-Pa, who had been watching this exchange, now climbed to his feet and went to Snefru. "Give me that," he said, snatching the clay pot out of Snefru's hands. "I worked as hard as you did today, and ache as much. I've earned it."

"I gave that to Snefru, not you," Imhotep said, also getting to his feet.

Tesh-Pa regarded him with amused contempt. "Well, it's mine now, snout," he said. "What are you going to do about it?"

Imhotep had no wish to get into a dispute with the hulking apprentice, and in any case was eager to be about his own business. But he couldn't let it go without saying something, so he made a crude suggestion involving a jackal and Tesh-Pa's mother. Tesh-Pa punched him in the belly, knocking the air out of him. Imhotep collapsed, gasping for breath. Grinning, Tesh-Pa walked away. Over his shoulder he said, "I may want more of this, snout. I'll let you know when you can give it to me."

Imhotep took a few moments longer to catch his breath, then slowly got to his feet, livid with fury. He clenched his fists and stalked after Tesh-Pa.

A pair of hands grabbed him from behind. Imhotep whirled around. It was Snefru. "Not like that," Snefru said. "That's exactly wrong."

"What?"

"You have tucked your thumb inside your fingers when you made a fist. You must keep it *outside*, else you're likely to break it if you hit someone hard enough."

Imhotep uncurled his fingers and stared at them. "Oh. I didn't know."

Snefru scoffed. "You don't do much fighting, do you?"

"Well, no."

Snefru glanced at Tesh-Pa, who was walking back to the chopping block. "We must return to our work now but meet me at the gate after work. I believe I can help you."

Lord Re's chariot was sliding down the western sky when Imhotep and Snefru met at the entrance to the abattoir grounds. They walked out into the street.

"You think you can help me best Tesh-Pa?"

"You certainly can't beat him in a fight the way things are now," said Snefru.

"Curse him, he took my gift to you. I have to stand up for what's right."

Snefru nodded slowly. "Yes, I like that about you. But you must learn to pick your fights. You take the Street of Crocodiles home, do you not? I go that way myself." The two boys began walking. "The problem with you is, you don't know how to tussle."

"I can hit. I've had people take advantage of me before, Snefru. I know how to handle myself."

"Scrapping with some child is one thing, but standing up

to an ill-tempered ox like Tesh-Pa is something else." Snefru scowled. "I am not schooled, like you…at least, not in the same way. I grew up on the streets of Mennefer and had to care for myself almost since I was able to walk."

"How did you feed yourself?"

Snefru shrugged. "I stole what I needed. Sometimes I got caught. Then they put me into the stocks."

"Oh." Imhotep had never personally known anyone who had been punished that way, by having wooden blocks secured around their feet. "I thought they only did that to criminals."

Snefru grinned for the first time, and his face was transformed. "What do you think I was? They shackled me at times too. I got tired of it and decided to learn how to do something useful that people would pay me for so that I wouldn't have to steal. I was always good with a knife, so I decided to put that skill to use. I practiced until I could use a knife better than anyone I knew. Then I hung around outside the abattoir, playing with my knife, balancing it on my fingers, spinning it around, until Ni-Ka-Re saw me demonstrating my talents for some of the other apprentices. He saw how well I could handle a blade and agreed to let me try slicing some meat. And here I am."

Imhotep grinned back. "I will make more of the salve for you." After a moment's thought, he said, "But I won't bring it here, lest Tesh-Pa snatch it again. I will leave it with a friend," he added, thinking of Meresankh, "and we will get it there."

Snefru smiled again. "Tomorrow after work, then, we will do a bit of brawling."

True to his word, the next afternoon Snefru took Imhotep to an alley not far from the abattoir. "Now let's have a look at you. Prepare to hit me." Snefru stepped back and examined Imhotep's stance. "You've got to keep your hands up to guard your face." He took hold of Imhotep's forearms. "Don't hold 'em down at your chest—no one can hurt you hitting you there, it's all bone. Keep 'em at chin level, like this." He lifted Imhotep's arms. "But you got to be ready to take one in the belly, so keep your left one down a bit to ward off a punch there."

Imhotep bit his lips. "Okay, like this?"

"Aye, perfect." Snefru began bobbing lightly on his feet. "Now I'm gonna throw a punch at you and you deflect it but come right back with one of your own. If you don't, it allows someone get in two or three more blows. You get me?"

"I do." The boys sparred for several minutes. Snefru usually got through Imhotep's guard, but he pulled his punches, so Imhotep sustained no further bruises.

"Your advantage is, you're tall with long arms," Snefru said. "You can get through anyone's guard with arms like those. So, what you do is this: you feint with the left…hook up toward the head…and you throw the right one across your opponent's face when he's trying to block that left. Like so." He demonstrated in the air before turning to Imhotep. "Now try that on me. Left… yeah, then right. Good!"

Over the next few days, Imhotep learned how to brawl, as Snefru called it. He learned how to punch or kick a foe to hurt him painfully or to make him too sick to continue; how to keep his chin tucked down to avoid being hit in the mouth; and when to duck his head to take a punch on the top of his skull rather than directly in the face.

"Now, some of the boys will come at you with a piece of pottery hidden in their hands, meaning to bash you or cut you with it. I know Tesh-Pa does that, so you got to watch out for it. Someone does that, you kick him good and hard like I showed you, yes? Right between the legs! That'll make him lose interest."

Imhotep nodded. "I want to practice some more. Don't pull your punches, Snefru. I need to understand the force involved and how best to deflect it."

"If you say so," Snefru said with obvious reluctance. Soon Imhotep had collected even more bruises, but Snefru admitted that he had learned how to keep his guard up, and how to throw an effective punch.

Sore but pleased with himself, Imhotep limped home.

Sebhot was sitting on a bench outside the doorway to their home. "By the sacred scrotum of Anubis! What's happened to you?"

Imhotep glanced inside to see if his mother or Wabet was within earshot. "Keep your voice down," he muttered. "A friend at work is teaching me how to fight."

Sebhot raised his eyebrows. "You're sure he is your friend?"

Kherry came outside. Her mouth fell open at the sight of Imhotep's contusions. "Ay-yi-yi! Your poor arms!"

"It's all right, Mother, really. I, uh, fell while carrying a basket of scraps."

He glanced at Sebhot, who rolled his eyes but said nothing.

She shook her head. "Some favor Ahmose has done us, finding you that job! You will become a beast."

Imhotep winced at her words. *Perhaps I already have. I am a beast of burden at work, and I am learning how to fight like a common ruffian.*

"Come, Tep," said Sebhot, "let's have a game of senet before supper." He tapped the well-worn box containing the game pieces and grinned at his brother.

Imhotep scoffed. "You always beat me, Seb! You always beat *every*one."

"I can't help it if I am good at the game."

"It's no fun if I lose all the time, but okay, just one."

"Very good!"

The following morning Imhotep stopped off at Rudjet's bakery on his way to work. Meresankh was arranging loaves of bread for display and grinned when she saw him approach. Despite the leap of his heart at the sight of her, he forced himself to sound businesslike. "Meresankh, would you do me a small favor?"

"Of course, I would, beloved. Anything you like."

Beloved! I like the sound of that. He took a small jar of unguent from his linen carry bag. "Would you keep this to one side for me? It's for a friend. I will come by after work today with him."

"Certainly," the girl said, taking the jar from him. When their fingers brushed, Imhotep felt a tingle. He strode to work feeling taller and half hoping that Tesh-Pa would pick a fight with him today. At the gate, however, he found two soldiers standing in conversation with Ni-Ka-Re. At his approach one of them gave him a cold stare but Ni-Ka-Re shook his head. "He works here. Imhotep, hurry; there is news. The royal guards wish to speak with all of us."

Now Imhotep saw all the workers standing in the small courtyard inside the gate instead of laboring at their tasks.

He walked over to Dhuti. "What's going on?"

"I'm not sure."

Imhotep looked over at Snefru, who shrugged. The apprentices whispered among themselves, trading guesses and rumors.

They didn't have long to wait. After everyone arrived, the soldiers thumped their spears on the ground for attention. One of them, a scarred man whose nose looked as if it had been broken more than once, spoke harshly. "Because this establishment provides meat for the king's table, you are all considered to be royal suppliers. Therefore you, too, may be in danger."

Imhotep's eyes went wide. Danger? The apprentices murmured among themselves.

"Silence!" barked the guard. "Early this morning while on rounds, a guard discovered the body of a priest outside the temple of Ptah. His throat had been slashed."

The workers gasped. "What? Slashed? Who could do such a thing?"

Imhotep could scarcely believe he had heard correctly. Such an act of murder would doom a man's *ka* to endless wandering through the Red Lands, the sweltering, rocky deserts of Kemet, friendless and without hope for all eternity. He shuddered. That this had been done to a priest was unthinkable.

The broken-nosed guard thumped the ground again. "The Sons of Atum committed this terrible crime."

Ni-Ka-Re loosed a string of pungent curses. The apprentices nodded and mumbled assent.

Imhotep could not help speaking aloud. "But I thought—"

"You thought *what?*" The guard scowled at him.

"That they...they were just a cult, harmless fools."

"Yes, many of us thought that as well. Apparently, we were wrong," he said. "They have become more aggressive, more ruthless. They mutilated the priest's corpse."

Imhotep's mouth fell open. This was even worse than murder. "Th-they dared do such a thing? But wait, honored one—how do you know it was the Sons?" He had heard his father mention the group, who were opposed to the rule of any god save Atum. They denied the superiority of Ptah and all other gods, claiming that Atum was the true creator of the universe and the only god who should rightly be worshipped. With unease, he remembered the ferryman who had taken him to his father's tomb mentioning the Sons of Atum being active in nearby Heliopolis.

Why were they now threatening cities north of the First Cataract? Worse, now they were taking lives.

The guard looked down his nose at Imhotep. "They left a note on a bloodstained piece of papyrus tied to the priest's arm, promising more killings unless their demands are met."

"W-what demands are these?" asked Ni-Ka-Re, wringing his hands.

"The immediate establishment of Atum as Supreme God in the Two Lands, the overthrow and destruction of Ptah's temple, and the removal of King Sanakhe from the throne in favor of a regent of their own choosing."

Ni-Ka-Re sputtered. "Absurd. King Sanakhe, may he live ten thousand years, will never agree to any of that."

Both guards nodded. "This is true," said the one with the broken nose, who had been doing all the talking. "He will not. But he's commanded all his subjects to be watchful. The Sons of Atum can be anywhere. They can strike anyone, at any time."

Snefru lifted his head. "You said that the priest's body was mutilated, honored one. In what way?"

"The mark of a snake was carved into his chest, and the note was signed with the same mark. The king commands you to be wary of strangers, especially those who seem to be from the south. If you see anything suspicious, report to the palace at once. Failure to do so may result in...unpleasant consequences for you."

With that, the soldiers departed.

No one could talk of anything else for the rest of the morning and through the noon meal. Imhotep, after the excitement was over, devoted himself to his work. The killing of a priest, shocking as it might be, after all had little to do with his own problems.

In the afternoon, news arrived that caused another stir. A messenger came for Ni-Ka-Re, who immediately called for Hori, the master butcher. Dhuti, who happened to be nearby when the runner made his appearance, loitered long enough outside Ni-Ka-Re's office to hear the message.

He went at once to Snefru and Imhotep. "You'll never guess!"

"Well, what is it?" Snefru asked. While Ni-Ka-Re was occupied with the runner, the apprentices paused in their labors.

"A friend of Ni-Ka-Re's is getting married," Dhuti said, "and has put in a big order!"

"I am surprised to learn that an ape like Ni-Ka-Re *has* friends," said Snefru with a grin. "What is the exalted one's name?"

"I hear it is Ahmose," said Dhuti.

"Ahmose!" exclaimed Imhotep.

"Just so," Dhuti replied.

Imhotep frowned. As the family of Kaneferw, Ahmose's former employer, he, his mother, and his brother would all be invited to the wedding festivities.

Now I will have to work on meat for his wedding feast, he thought.

On the other hand, perhaps I can learn something of what he's been up to.

"So, Ahmose is getting himself married, eh?" Snefru spat to one side. "I can't imagine who'd marry him."

"You know him, then?" Imhotep leaned against a wall, making a show of examining the blood caked under his nails.

"That rat? Not really. He has come here to visit Ni-Ka-Re a few times. I don't like his manner. He thinks he is better than us, just because his friend runs the place."

Dhuti grinned, showing gaps in his teeth. "That *does* make him better than us, you dolt." Even Snefru laughed at this.

"I hear he bought his wife-to-be a necklace from the shop of Amenemhet the goldsmith." Dhuti bit at his nails. Like Imhotep's, they were dark with the blood caked under them. Imhotep looked away.

Tesh-Pa, standing nearby, whistled. "Amenemhet is the finest goldsmith in all of Mennefer."

Dhuti nodded. "Had it made special, they say. I didn't think he was rich enough for Amenemhet's services."

That's what I would have thought too. Yet here he is getting married, buying much meat, and gifting his bride-to-be with gold, Imhotep thought. *Interesting.*

The gossip continued even after they returned to work, but Imhotep took no further part in it. His heart buzzed like the flies around him.

Hori trundled, scowling, out of Ni-Ka-Re's inner sanctum and gestured for Imhotep. "The noble Weshptah has ordered a cow to be butchered today, had you forgotten? Come, we must get to work at once."

Imhotep wanted to ask about Ahmose's upcoming feast but knew that Hori would say nothing about that. He therefore fell to his duties with the vessels for capturing blood, and, after the cow was dispatched, he helped dismember its carcass.

He didn't mind being busy, for by now he had learned enough about his job to carry out the required tasks without needing to think much about them.

The mention of the goldsmith Amenemhet sparked Imhotep's memory. The golden jewelry his parents had worn at their wedding had been made by Amenemhet. Kaneferw enjoyed surprising his wife with gifts of jewelry, which delighted her, but she specially prized those from Amenemhet. The memory brought a smile to Imhotep's face as he remembered the bracelets in the box in the basement. Then he scowled. Those bracelets had paid for Kaneferw's funeral. He brought his knife down on a joint with unnecessary force.

Things came suddenly together in his heart, as neatly as a list of numbers: Ahmose's fake injury (whack); the lack of money in the atelier coffers (chop); Ahmose's shady companions (crunch); and his newfound wealth (hack). *There is a connection*, Imhotep told himself. *My heart knows that Ahmose has something to do with the ledger figures that will not add up.* The strip of burned papyrus on which Odji had drawn the mysterious symbol had been burned in a fire. It *could* be from a secret ledger.

But why would Ahmose have secret ledgers in the first place? Imhotep could think of no reason. He could not believe that his father had known of them or was engaged in cheating his customers. He *would* not believe it. But Ahmose—well, that was different, somehow, especially now that unsavory aspects of Ahmose's personality were coming to light. Even though there was, as of yet, no clear-cut evidence of deliberate wrongdoing on Ahmose's part, Imhotep could not rid himself of a growing suspicion that the lead apprentice was up to something. Thinking of Odji's burned scrap of papyrus, Imhotep thought: *He has destroyed evidence. But evidence of what? There must be more clues somewhere.*

It all sounded like some hard-to-believe fictional tale, but Imhotep was certain of its truth. Now he had to prove that his notions were based on fact. He needed proof.

His thoughts were interrupted when Hori handed him a spherical stone hammer. "Crack the skull," he said to Imhotep. "You may share the brains with the others."

Imhotep took the tool, gazing at the animal's bloodstained head. He had not committed this act before. It was, he knew, something of an honor. "I thank you," he said. "Dhuti? Will you catch its brains for me?"

"I will." The other apprentice positioned himself with a catchment bowl.

Imhotep hefted the hammer and then swung it. The skull cracked without needing a second blow. He watched the brains leak into the bowl, wishing he were Ma'at and able to judge the balance of truth in the animal's heart. *I would have the truth in Ahmose's heart. Yes, somehow, I will uncover it.*

Frustration surged through him like pent-up water into an irrigation canal, pouring into his heart and leaving room for nothing else. He closed his eyes and raised his head skyward. *A sign is all I ask of you, Thoth. You have convinced me that these things mean something. But what?*

The ibis-headed god, however, provided no sign. Imhotep's thoughts circled around Ahmose's supposed injury, his wedding, the expensive gold bracelet, and Odji's suspicions of Mekure, the late-night visitor with his strangely marked foot. And the mark on Ahmose's own foot.

What did it all mean?

"Imhotep! Back to work!" Ni-Ka-Re yelled, interrupting Imhotep's musings. "See to salting the mutton."

"I obey."

He blinked and sat up straight, no longer seeing the pits or the buzzing flies. Instead, he saw Ahmose's face.

Slowly he resumed placing the meat into the natron pit. The more he thought about it, the more sense it made. Ahmose—it had all been Ahmose.

He was with my father when he died. We suddenly have no money, and now he does. Father's death wasn't an accident. Ahmose did it. He killed my father for his wealth. I am sure of it—but I cannot prove it! He has put me here to keep me out of his way. I will tell everyone what I know to be true!

He bit his lip. *No, Imhotep—they will say that you are chasing birds. They will say that you are dreaming while you are awake.*

But he didn't believe he was.

Lord Thoth, if ever I needed a sign that I am having truthful thoughts, it is now. He prepared himself for a message from the god. Yet as before, no message or sign came.

Disheartened and white from the itchy natron dust, he returned to work.

After the day's labors were completed, Imhotep went with Snefru to the bakery where Meresankh greeted him cheerfully and fetched the pot of unguent he had given her. Snefru accepted it gladly. As they were leaving, he said to Imhotep, "She's a pretty one, isn't she?"

"Yes, she is."

"You *like* her, don't you?"

Imhotep looked askance at his friend. "I do, and we have pledged our troth to marry soon."

Snefru nodded. "You are a lucky fellow, Imhotep."

That night as he lay on his pallet staring up at the stars, Imhotep once more begged Thoth for a sign that his suspicions were true. *If I know this, then I will know how to proceed, and what to do. I mean, I do not know now—but it will become clear because I will know the truth of it.*

He squeezed his eyes shut so hard that he saw lights and opened his heart fully to the sky. Nut, goddess of the sky, spangled the heavens with stars each night while Re's sun boat journeyed elsewhere. Thoth, whose domain was the moon, also came to prominence as the stars came out.

Something to Imhotep's left caught his attention. He held his breath as a bright light crossed the sky in utter silence, growing smaller as it went until it vanished in the west. He had seen falling stars before, but never such a large one. Some said that they were a god traveling to earth, like Lord Re in his boat, or Thoth himself in a curved slice of the moon; others insisted that stupendous battles between demons above the sky occasionally knocked a star loose from its place.

Whatever the case, Imhotep knew that this falling star was

the sign he had sought. Thoth, pleased with his prayers, had answered them with confirmation.

Imhotep lay back, satisfied and calm in his heart for the first time in many days. *From now on, Ahmose had better be very careful, for I will know the truth of it all.*

12

Three days later came the Festival of Hedjihotep, goddess of weaving. It was a minor celebration, but for Imhotep it meant a day off from the abattoir. He moped around the house for a while, poking into this and that, unable to get Ahmose off his heart. At last Sebhot threw down the scroll he was trying to read. "By Anubis! You prowl around here like a starving dog. Will you not go visit Hau or find some other way to productively occupy yourself?"

"I'm sorry, I know I am restless." He made a face. "What I'd like to do is to take Father's ledgers to Chancellor Pepi and have *him* go over them. Perhaps we are too close to the problem, Seb. Maybe a fresh pair of eyes is what we need."

"Then by all means, *take* the cursed things and go; give us all some peace for a while." He picked up his senet case. "I am going to see if I can find someone who will play a game with me."

Imhotep gathered up the papyrus ledger scrolls and left the house. Across the street he saw a young, thin-faced man, a stranger to the neighborhood, loitering at the corner. He didn't take any particular notice of the fellow, but halfway to Pepi's house a sudden sneeze caused him to drop one of the scrolls. When he bent to pick it up, he noticed the same fellow following along half a block behind him. The man turned left at the next corner. Imhotep tried to shrug his presence off as a mere coincidence. *Come*, he chided himself, *you really are imagining things*. But he couldn't quite convince himself.

The chancellor's home was several streets farther on. Odji's sister, Noha, received him at the door and let him in. She looked sullen and unkempt, with dark circles under her eyes.

"Are you well?" Imhotep asked, thinking he might be able to

provide her with a potion made from the red berries with which
he had revived his mother's flagging spirit.

She looked up at him sadly. "I would be, but Pepi...favors
me." A tear trickled down her cheek. "I do not like what he has
me do."

"He is cruel to you?" It wasn't uncommon in the city for
people to take pleasure in mistreating their slaves.

"Nnnno. Not the way you think." She would supply no details, but Imhotep, having discussed Noha's plight with Odji,
was sure he knew why she was disconsolate. Many men abused
their female slaves, but all Noha would say was, "These are not
our customs. In my homeland I would be dishonored. Dis-
graced, even." She sighed. "In some ways it is fortunate that I
am *not* home."

"Your brother Odji is concerned about you," Imhotep said.

"Please tell him I am well, and miss him very much," Noha
said, looking sadder than ever.

"I will."

At that moment Chancellor Pepi stepped out of his office
and strode down the hall. He waved Noha away without a
glance. "Imhotep! This is an unexpected pleasure."

"Thank you, Your Honor," Imhotep replied. "I have come
to seek your advice."

"Of course, of course." Pepi conducted him into his office.
Like Kaneferw's workspace in the atelier, it was crowded with
papyrus manuscripts and writing implements. Pepi, a longtime
legal scholar, listened gravely as Imhotep outlined the situation
regarding Kaneferw's finances and his suspicions about Ahmose.

"These are serious matters," Pepi said when Imhotep was
finished. "What would you have me do?"

"I know it's much to ask, but would you examine the ledgers? Sebhot and I have worked in the atelier with our father, of
course, but the accounts were always primarily his responsibility
and Ahmose's. Everything seems accounted for, but we could
have missed something."

"Of course," said Pepi, taking the scrolls. "But you must give me some time to look them over." He cocked his head to one side. "You are making allegations against Ahmose. That is serious. You claim to have witnessed him using his hand without trouble. Did anyone *else* see this?"

Imhotep wanted to tell him that Odji had seen Ahmose using his supposedly injured hand—but Odji was a slave, and his testimony would carry little weight. "Not as such, no. We can ask for the opinion of a professional healer, if my testimony is not enough."

"Do not run away with yourself. Now, we can prove that Ahmose is a liar because he is faking a serious injury when he has none; but you allege that he is implicated in your father's death. That is a very serious accusation, you know."

"I do know. I also know that I do not have proof."

Pepi remained silent for some time, thinking. "What I would like to do," he said at last, "is to attack this problem from two angles: from the financial side, and from the physical. Your testimony about his arm will suffice for the latter, I believe. You are of good character and are known to the community through your father, whose own character was unimpeachable. For the former, however, we need more. If we can prove Ahmose has falsified your father's books, we can then discover what he has done with the money. Because, you see, surely he did what he did for a reason. Eh? I am interested in these friends of his of whom you speak. I will look into their backgrounds at court to see if they are mentioned in other criminal proceedings."

"Thank you," said Imhotep, gratefully. "I am much in your debt."

"We shall see. There is a great deal of work yet to do." Pepi scowled. "For the time being, say nothing to anyone about our discussion. I wonder…"

"You wonder what?"

"I wonder if Ahmose were to find out that he is under investigation, would he grow careless and make more mistakes." Pepi shook his head. "I will think on this. Come see me in two

days and we will talk. Meanwhile, enjoy the rest of the festival."
Imhotep bowed and took his leave.

ॐ

Following the goddess of weaving's festival, the abattoir
hummed with activity as the workers hurried to catch up with
the schedule of butchery. Imhotep had by this time become an
effective and relatively efficient worker. He threaded his way
easily through the press of apprentices, pleased with his ability
to juggle tasks and contribute to the daily assignments.

On the second day following the festival, however, Imhotep,
distracted by thoughts of Ahmose's doings and anxious to find
out what Chancellor Pepi might have learned, collided with
Tesh-Pa, who dropped the basket of bloody ribs he carried.
Imhotep stood stupidly, brought back to reality by the impact.

Ni-Ka-Re, seeing only Tesh-Pa scrambling in the dirt for the
ribs, vigorously applied his lash to the burly apprentice's shoulders. "Now wash those off!" Ni-Ka-Re stalked away, cursing
and shaking his head. Rubbing his bloodied wounds, Tesh-Pa
leveled a furious stare at Imhotep.

"I will see you this afternoon after work. Don't you dare
flee."

Imhotep's heart sank and he went cold. Other apprentices
nearby had heard the threat, and they whispered among themselves as the news spread.

Snefru sidled up next to him as the enraged apprentice lum-
bered off. "So, your first chance at a real brawl!"

"I would rather avoid it," Imhotep muttered.

"Oh, you can't do that," said Snefru, chortling. "He'd simply
wait for you outside tomorrow morning. No, you've got to fight
him."

"I suppose so, but you don't have to sound so *pleased* about
it."

"Never mind, never mind. All you have to do is to remember
what I've taught you." He leaned closer and glanced around.
"Most of all, you must be careful of his feet. He likes to kick,

and he's good at it. He'll try to kick you in the groin or the face first thing. You've got to watch out for that."

"Thanks. I just wish he didn't have so many people rooting for him."

Snefru snorted. "No one likes the big baboon; but he's so ill-tempered and mean that it pays to stay on his good side. Believe me, if it weren't you, it'd be someone else."

"*That's* not much consolation," Imhotep said dismally.

After work all the apprentices gathered outside the gate to watch the fight. Imhotep did his best to remain completely impassive, even disinterested, though his stomach felt ready to expel his last meal.

Tesh-Pa stamped around, shouting insults and threats. "Snout! You spawn of a crippled hippo! I will tear your nose off your face and replace it with a *real* snout, from the lowliest pig I can find!"

Imhotep quailed inwardly, but allowed himself a slight smile that he knew would infuriate Tesh-Pa. *If I can get him mad enough,* Imhotep thought, *he'll be less careful.* "I have seen roosters do this before they fight," he said. "Crow and strut. Much noise to little effect."

Several of the apprentices tittered. Sure enough, the bigger youth's face went dark red at the taunt.

"You think you're smarter than I am, eh, you pimply snout?"

The insult rankled, but Imhotep, refusing to show his irritation, kept the provoking smirk on his face.

One of the onlookers sang out, "*Everyone* thinks he's smarter than you!" Tesh-Pa whirled around to see who it was, but the voice had been disguised in a girlish pitch.

"Just you wait, whoever you are," Tesh-Pa said. "I'll find you out after I take care of this insect." He faced Imhotep and dropped into a crouch.

Imhotep, remembering Snefru's warning, flexed his knees. Tesh-Pa drew back his fist as if preparing for a blow, but kicked out instead, aiming for Imhotep's face. Imhotep ducked, caught the foot in both hands, and yanked up as hard as he could, using Tesh-Pa's speed and weight against him. The big apprentice crashed back into the ground, his head hitting with a thump. Imhotep, prepared to let him rise, saw how dazed he was and stepped back.

"No, no, no, take him, take him!" Snefru hopped up and down with excitement. "Don't let him get up."

Tesh-Pa levered himself up on his elbows. "You dog, you stinking hyena!"

Imhotep nodded once at Snefru, then stepped forward, onto Tesh-Pa's chest, forcing him down and pushing the air out of him. He dropped to his knees and put his left forearm across Tesh-Pa's throat, making it difficult for the bigger youth to draw a breath. Slowly Tesh-Pa's face turned even redder. The apprentice gathered himself, but Imhotep was ready for an attack. Tesh-Pa's arms flew up, but Imhotep wriggled to one side and grabbed the apprentice's left hand. He bent the little finger back until it snapped.

Tesh-Pa's eyes went wide. He howled in pain. Imhotep stood and brushed himself off as his antagonist writhed in the mud. He felt light-headed yet powerful, as though liquid sunlight were coursing through his body. The onlookers cheered and whistled, chanting, "Im-ho-tep! Im-ho-tep!"

Imhotep acknowledged their accolades with a nod and a smile. At a sound behind him, he turned to see Tesh-Pa clambering to his feet, cradling his injured hand.

"That was well done," he said, managing a lopsided grin. "Very well done." He turned to the others. "This man, this is Imhotep! He is my friend. Anyone messing with him will have to talk to me." He gripped Imhotep's forearm with his good hand.

Imhotep glanced at Snefru, who winked at him. Imhotep resisted the temptation to show off or brag. He had humiliated the bully, who had immediately declared them friends rather than admit to the shame of being bested by a weaker foe. *I can hurt as well as heal*, Imhotep thought. *I had never thought of this before.*

Imhotep bound Tesh-Pa's finger, using a straight stick under the dressing to keep it immobile. The process must have caused Tesh-Pa considerable pain, but he gritted his teeth and made no outcry, though perspiration poured down his face.

He sat looking curiously at the dressing when Imhotep was through. "Why the stick?"

"That way your finger won't be crooked when it's healed."

Tesh-Pa shook his head. "Hmph. You are wise in healing ways. If you're a healer, what are you doing here, cutting meat and mopping up blood?"

That was a good question. Imhotep pondered it as he walked home, ignoring the clamor of life in the streets around him.

I would have been better off at the atelier, and if we had had work that is where I'd be.

And yet he had learned much in the butcher shop, and his strength had improved. He had made new friends. So perhaps it was for the best after all.

"Eh, eh…you should watch where you are going."

Imhotep blinked. Hau stood before him on the street, his rheumy old eyes twinkling.

"Master, I pray your pardon. I did not see you."

"You all but knocked me down," said Hau. "What is filling your thoughts? That young baker girl?"

Imhotep felt his face grow red. "No, not her." He drew a deep breath. "I am on my way to speak with Chancellor Pepi." He took Hau aside and swiftly explained his suspicions concerning Ahmose and his possible tampering with Kaneferw's finances.

As Hau listened his face grew more serious. When Imhotep was finished, he said, "These are serious matters. You have not made any open accusations, have you?"

"No. Pepi cautioned me not to do so while he made inquiries. His words will guide me."

"Hmmm. You must be very careful."

"I will, you may rely on that."

When Imhotep arrived at Pepi's home, Noha guided him

into the chancellor's office. Preoccupied though he was with his own concerns, Imhotep nevertheless noticed that the girl looked less harried. *Hopefully she has been able to avoid her master's more predatory attentions*, he thought. He rather wished he didn't need Pepi's assistance, but the man had been a trusted family friend ever since Imhotep could remember. He pushed his guilt to one side. "Have you learned anything that may help me?" he asked the older man, who waved him to a carved wooden chair.

"Nothing conclusive, but it seems that through his own family, Ahmose has connections to political factions in the south."

Imhotep sat straighter in his chair. "The Sons of Atum have prominence in the south."

"Precisely so. Now! What I have done is summon Ahmose here today for an unofficial interview. He knows I am connected with your family, and I have told him I want to discuss certain matters with him. Being as how I am helping to look after your mother, and he was your father's most intimate business associate, he cannot easily refuse."

"That makes sense."

"Yes, and you will be listening—but not directly. I believe he will speak more freely if he does not know you are present. My hope is that he will be enough at ease to perhaps let something slip. It might be something subtle enough that I will not notice it, which is why I want your ears as well as my own." A clamor at the front door caught their attention.

"That will be Ahmose," said Pepi. He pointed to a curtained alcove where he kept racks of scrolls. "Hide yourself in there."

Imhotep slid behind the curtain and made himself as comfortable as he could. Moments later Noha conducted Ahmose into the room.

"Chancellor," Ahmose snapped. "I'm very busy getting ready for my marriage. What exactly was it that you wanted to see me about?"

"I thought my message made it clear," Pepi said mildly. Imhotep heard him tap his finger on the pile of papyrus scrolls on his desk. "I am concerned for the family of my late friend Kaneferw. They have been left almost poverty-stricken in the wake of his death, and I wish to understand how this could have happened. Before Kaneferw died, it's my understanding that his business was doing quite well. Well enough that he had granted his eldest son two months to pursue his studies in healing in the countries to the south. Yet so much has gone awry for the family that Imhotep has had to take a position in your friend's abattoir in order to provide food for his mother and brother."

Imhotep heard a sound that he interpreted as Ahmose crossing his legs. "I felt fortunate to be able to offer the family assistance in that way."

"It will weigh in your favor on the scales of Ma'at," said Pepi. Imhotep heard a scroll being unrolled on Pepi's desk. "I have been going over Kaneferw's ledgers, as I say, and I have found some discrepancies. These, I note, are marked in your hand."

Imhotep sat up straighter. *So Sebhot and I were right. Ahmose did tamper with the records! That rat.*

"I have no doubt of it," said Ahmose, who did not sound in the least put out or guilty. "You will see that the entries were all made around the time of Kaneferw's death. I was rattled by his loss and pained by my injuries. Much responsibility fell on me, Chancellor. I was not used to it and there were so many things I suddenly had to do. Commissions to handle, clients to notify, creditors to pay… I knew that I had made errors. I did what I could to rectify them. I copied out certain portions of the ledgers, finding it easier to work on sections. Then, when I was done with them, I burned the copies to prevent more confusion."

There was silence for a few moments. Imhotep clenched his fists. Ahmose had admitted destroying what could be evidence. What would Pepi say?

"Your actions skirt the edges of the law," the chancellor

said at last. "I understand that you had good intentions, but you must also know that for tax purposes it's illegal to destroy records, even copies of them."

"I understand." Ahmose sounded chastened. "Chancellor, if I may? I have errands to run, due to my wedding—"

"Of course, of course; I understand. Be off with you and we will talk later."

Imhotep heard Ahmose rise and depart the room. A few moments later he heard the front door open and close. Pepi pulled back the curtain and Imhotep stepped into the room.

"You heard," said Pepi. "He claims confusion and readily admits his errors. He does not sound like a guilty man."

"Yet we know he has been lying about his arm. Which reminds me—I couldn't see him through the curtain. Is he still wearing a sling?"

"He is."

"So we know he is still lying about that at least."

"Yes, but being a liar is not the same as being a murderer or an embezzler." Pepi pursed his lips. "Here is what I can do. He cannot refuse an order from me to appear in court to discuss his altering of the ledgers. After his wedding, I will summon him. He may well confess during interrogation, and between now and then we may be able to learn more about his doings. How does that sound?"

Imhotep bowed his head. "Thank you, sir." He took his leave, not entirely satisfied, but pleased that something, at least, was being done.

13

Hori commonly did the killing of cattle whose meat was meant for the royal table, but it was the job of Unas to handle animals destined to feed minor nobles or wealthy commoners. Unas usually dispatched two or three cows per day, and then helped cut them up. Imhotep was busy removing innards when he heard a commotion from the back of the compound. As he looked up he heard a scream, then the bellowing of a bull and much shouting.

"What—?"

Ni-Ka-Re ran from the rear. "Imhotep, you know something of healing."

"Well, yes, but—"

Ni-Ka-Re grabbed his shoulder, yanked him to his feet. "Unas has been gored."

Unas lay in the bloody mud, his hands pressed to his belly as blood welled between his fingers. The bull had been roped and led away. Unas's cries filled the air. Imhotep saw at once that this was a very bad wound, one that Hau himself might well have shaken his head over. Hau had taught that there were three levels of illness or injury: "One I will treat, one with which I will contend, and one which is not to be treated." Meaning, as he'd explained, diagnoses of favorable, uncertain, and unfavorable.

Unas's injury looked unfavorable. Imhotep could see pink intestines showing through the torn flesh and the blood. And there were no medical materials here.

He turned to Ni-Ka-Re. "Pray, find a healer nearby, explain what happened. I will try to help him."

The apprentices stood about, white-faced. Imhotep looked up at them. "I need a cloth, something, anything. Tesh-Pa, help me lift him up onto a table. We've got to get him out of the mud."

Tesh-Pa, still favoring the hand Imhotep had injured, stepped forward to assist. Imhotep bent over Unas. "A cloth, a cloth. Set take you all, has no one a cloth?"

The apprentices glanced at each other. Snefru, who was marginally less filthy than the others, stripped off his loincloth and handed it to Imhotep.

"It will do." He wrapped it around Unas's belly, but it was instantly soaked with blood. *Thoth help me—this will not work. The wound is too large.*

Unas grasped Imhotep's forearms. "I can see it…the West! I see green fields and a great light…my father…my—" And he was gone.

Imhotep gazed down at the man in sorrow, wishing he could have helped him. He breathed a prayer to Ma'at that she would find him worthy to join his ancestors.

೩

Around mid-morning the next day, Imhotep paused while cutting up a sheep haunch to wipe his forearm across his perspiring brow. The movement smeared blood on his face but he was long past any fastidious feelings he had had when he first started at the abattoir. Glancing toward the abattoir gate, he saw Ni-Ka-Re arrive, accompanied by a burly man of about thirty-five, with big teeth and a lazy eye. Imhotep recognized him at once.

Kagemni? Now what is he *doing here?* Kagemni, who had worked for Kaneferw as a construction foreman, had been on site at the royal summer house site in the Fayum where Kaneferw had lost his life. According to Ahmose, Kagemni had stayed there to supervise while Ahmose accompanied Kaneferw's body back to Mennefer. Imhotep had not known he had returned. Broad-shouldered and thick-necked, he made even the beefy Tesh-Pa look like a stripling.

Imhotep raised his hand to acknowledge the crew leader. To his surprise Kagemni made no response, his eyes passing over him incuriously as he inspected the apprentices.

I am so smeared with filth that he does not recognize me; and perhaps I am taller and more muscular as well. He would have gone over to the man, but he suspected that would result in a lash, so he kept at his work. At the noontime meal break, he approached Ni-Ka-Re.

"I saw you conducting Kagemni on a tour of the premises. He worked for my father. What was he doing here?"

Ni-Ka-Re stared at him for a moment, and Imhotep realized he might have overstepped his bounds. "We must replace Unas, if it's any of your business. Kagemni came to apply for a job slaughtering cows. He has not had work, he says, since your father's architecture studio closed. He did not say that he saw you."

"Will you hire him?" Imhotep did his best to make the question casual, of no consequence.

"I believe so. He is strong and not of a squeamish nature. He will do well with the cattle. Is he a reliable man?"

"Yes, most reliable."

Ni-Ka-Re grunted. "I wish more workers here were like that."

Imhotep took the hint and returned to his labors.

The next day it happened that he arrived for work at the same time as Kagemni. "Luck, luck, luck to you on your first day here," said Imhotep, using the common form of wishing good fortune in morning, afternoon, and evening.

Kagemni looked uncomfortable. "I, uh, yes. Thank you." He brushed past Imhotep and hurried through the gate. Imhotep stared after the foreman. This was a man who had always been friendly to him, who had gone out of his way to show Imhotep around construction sites and explain methods of building. Kagemni had taught him how to split a stone using a hammer and a chisel, and how to use a plumb to establish a straight vertical line. He'd known Kagemni since he was a small child, had eaten with him at the same table. Now the man acted almost like a stranger.

Puzzled, Imhotep bent to his work.

During the noon meal, Imhotep ate with Tash-Pa, Dhuti, and Snefru. Kagemni came out from the slaughter area to the rear and sat down by himself to eat.

Dhuti chewed a date. "What's with that fellow? He's watching us."

Imhotep glanced at Kagemni.

Snefru said, "Not *us*... I think he's watching Imhotep. I've seen him a few times today, when he comes out to talk to Ni-Ka-Re. He always looks toward Imhotep. Tep, you said you know him?"

Imhotep shrugged. "He worked for my father. He used to be friendly, but no longer. I don't know...perhaps he blames me for losing his job."

"You had nothing to do with that," said Tesh-Pa. He stuffed a piece of bread into his mouth, chewed it, and swallowed. "I mean, from what *you've* said, he was at the site where your father was killed, was he not?"

Imhotep blinked. *That's correct, he was. I wonder if he knows anything about Ahmose?* Aloud, he said, "Yes. I don't know what his problem is." He shrugged, pretending nonchalance. "I'll ask him about it."

He dawdled while the others returned to work. Seeing Kagemni still eating, Imhotep rose and approached him. "Greetings, Kagemni. How are you faring?"

"Well enough, boy."

Taken aback by the man's cold tone and the deliberate insult, Imhotep said, "I...I was happy to see you find new work. Doubtless it was through Ahmose?"

Kagemni stood and brushed himself off. "How I found it is not your concern. Now tend to your tasks and I will tend to mine." He walked away.

For the rest of the day Imhotep often noticed Kagemni gazing at him while he worked. The big man's stony stare made him feel uncomfortable. Imhotep, for his part, tried to watch Kagemni as well, but wielding a sharp knife to cut meat required all of his attention, so he was not able to spend much time observing the man.

Shortly before the end of the workday, Imhotep was on an errand near the slaughtering area. A cow had been brought in for the kill and was being manhandled into position by several apprentices. Kagemni, wielding a large hammer, waited patiently. The cow's eyes rolled in apprehension. It lunged for freedom, knocking Kagemni off his feet, exposing his soles.

Imhotep, watching, gasped. On the bottom of Kagemni's foot was a mark.

That evening Odji came to Imhotep's home for a reading lesson. "My master has gone out with his friends again," he said. "He won't be back anytime soon." He handed Imhotep a piece of pottery.

"What's this? Another marking from someone's foot?"

"Yes."

"Hmmm. A simple circle. That doesn't tell us much." Yet he had the tantalizing feeling that this was something he should recognize. "Listen, Odji. Can you describe the man who had this one?" He drew the mark he'd seen on Kagemni's foot on another piece of pottery.

 "Certainly. He is a very big man, sour of expression, with an eye that looks off to one side and teeth that stick out, like this." He demonstrated, pulling in his lower lip.

"I see." Kagemni—it had to be. Of course, the simple fact that he was a drinking friend of Ahmose's really meant nothing… But a great deal of circumstantial evidence was piling up. "And the man with the one you've just brought me?"

Odji shrugged. "Short, stocky…big in the chest and arms. Looks rather like a baboon."

Imhotep rubbed his chin. That could be a description of Ni-Ka-Re. Well, somehow there had to be a way of discovering whether the abattoir's overseer had the mark on his foot. He'd see about that on the morrow. If it turned out to be true, that meant that three men associated with one another—Ahmose, Ni-Ka-Re, and Kagemni—bore strange marks on their feet. Signifying…what, exactly?

It could be a coincidence that they all have odd tattoos on their feet… but somehow, I do not think it is.

After Odji left, Imhotep drew the four symbols on a blank area of the papyrus-leaf journal he kept under his sleeping pallet. He stared at them, knowing they held a secret for him if only he were wise enough to decipher it.

They're not hieroglyphs, nor pictures of anything I recognize. He shuffled them around, rearranging their relative positions vertically as well as horizontally, but could make nothing of the puzzle.

If I can get one more clue, I'm sure I will have it.

He thought back to Kagemni, watching him all day at work, keeping an eye on him—

"By Thoth! An *eye!* That's it!" In his journal he drew the signs he had already seen and added new ones to make a composite picture:

Odji's "symbols" were simply segments of the wadjet: the Eye of Re. The goddess Wadjet was one of the oldest deities of the Two Lands. She was the personification of Ta-Mehu, Lower Kemet, the region stretching north from Mennefer to the delta country where the Nile split into many rivers emptying into the great Green Sea.

Furthermore, she was a daughter of Ptah's ancient aspect, Atum—

Imhotep gasped. *The daughter of Atum.*

He stared out across the darkness, seeing only the flaming eye of Wadjet. The daughter of Atum…could there be a connection here with the *Sons* of Atum, who were spreading terror and fear throughout the population?

In the Temple of Ptah, Imhotep had learned that Wadjet was one of the goddesses called "Eye of Re," along with Bast, Sekhmet, Hathor, and Tefnut. They were all charged with watching over the doings of mankind. She had been the first to earn the honorific, when she was sent to find Tefnut and Shu, the Lord of Light, when they were lost in the waters of the primordial sea, Nun.

All well and good…but Wadjet, on Atum's orders, had almost caused the destruction of mankind when Atum decided that humans were not as respectful of him as they should be. A trick fooled her, saving humanity.

Angrily he waved away the old stories. His problems were current, of immediate concern. Kagemni and Ahmose, and probably Ni-Ka-Re, all bore tattoos, sections of the Eye of Wadjet. But why not the entire Eye? What did it all mean?

One thing it probably meant was that there were other men bearing the remaining two segments of the eye of Wadjet, the ones he had not yet seen:

Six men, then, at least, joined together in an association having something to do with the Sons of Atum. Imhotep drew into himself, feeling chilly in the cool night air. His heart whirled, thoughts dancing, but he could tease no thread out of the strange facts. At last he fell asleep.

Upon awakening in the morning he took another look at the drawing he'd made the night before. In the clear light of day the whole idea seemed absurd, laughable. Tattoos on feet connecting to terrorists?

Yet he could not rid himself of the conviction that he had stumbled on important clues. *I need help fitting them together*, he thought. *I will speak to Chancellor Pepi about it this very day.*

He gobbled breakfast and set out for Pepi's home. As he left the house, he saw a man across the street. *That fellow looks familiar*, he thought, but had no time to hail him. Halfway to Pepi's home he realized when he had seen the man before: on the occasion he had gone to discuss the tattoos with Pepi, two days earlier.

He is following me, Imhotep thought, but when he looked for the thin-faced young man he was nowhere to be seen. *I do not have time to look for him now.* He took a step toward Pepi's dwelling, then stopped. *I will make the time! He cannot have gone far.* Fleet of foot, Imhotep dashed up and down the nearest streets and in a short time spotted the man walking hurriedly toward the center of the city.

Impulsively, Imhotep collided with him, knocking him over.

"Your pardon," he gasped. "I am late for work!" He ran off, but not before glimpsing a mark on the bottom of the man's foot: *I knew it!*

Before long he stood panting at Pepi's gate. "Chancel-

lor!" he called through the gate. "It's Imhotep. I must see you."

A few moments passed. He shifted from one foot to the other, waiting. Someone inside hurriedly approached the gate.

When she appeared, he recognized Noha, a new bruise coloring her face. Avoiding Imhotep's eyes, she stepped aside and motioned for him to enter.

"The chancellor is having his breakfast in the courtyard," she said as he passed.

"Thanks, Noha. I know where it is."

She retreated into the house. Imhotep walked through to the inner courtyard. Pepi sat on a stool near his garden, attended by two young female slaves. He held a scroll in one hand and an olive in the other. Seeing Imhotep, he popped the olive in his mouth, chewed, and spat the stone onto the pavement, from which one of the girls impassively plucked it.

Pepi has no male slaves. Why have I never noticed this?

"Ah, Imhotep! Will you take some refreshment with me?"

"Yes, thank you."

Pepi spoke to one of the slave girls, who hurried off to fetch a stool.

"I'm on my way to work but I wanted to ask you about Ahmose. Have you spoken with him?"

"Indeed, I have." Pepi selected another olive from the bowl before him. He ate it, again spitting out the stone. The stool arrived and Imhotep settled himself while Pepi ate more olives. Imhotep took a date from a bowl.

"I have nothing new to report to you about Ahmose," Pepi said, "if that's what is on your heart."

"I have something else to discuss, however, if you have time." Imhotep reached into his lunch bag and brought out the page of his journal with the drawings. He explained the markings Odji had seen on the feet of Ahmose's associates, and his own conviction that when combined they were meant to form an Eye of Wadjet.

"And I feel that somehow they tie into the Sons of Atum, the goddess being a *daughter* of Atum."

Pepi rubbed his chin, staring at the drawing. "And you say that Kagemni, Ni-Ka-Re, and Ahmose all bear these tattooed markings?"

"That is correct, as does a thin young man who was following me this morning, on my way here. I tripped him up and saw this mark on his foot." He traced the upper curve of the eye.

"Hmmm." Pepi stood, and paced back and forth for some moments, a grave expression on his face. "I must tell you something, in strictest confidence."

"Of course, Chancellor. You know you can trust me."

Pepi nodded. "Yes, I do know that." He blew out his breath. "What's more important, I know your father trusted you as well, else I would not share what I know. You are young, but your heart works well." He kept pacing, frowning thoughtfully for a while before speaking again. "A few months before your father died, he and I and a number of other citizens were called to the palace by Prince Djoser. This was at the time of the spring equinox, just before the harvest festival. Perhaps you remember him being away from the atelier then?"

"He was often away, on a job site, or at a meeting with some patron or another." Imhotep shrugged. "Occasionally I accompanied him, often I did not."

"Yes, well, in this instance he would not have had you along, because the meeting with Djoser was meant to be secret. He never mentioned it to you?"

Imhotep shook his head.

"Good. A fine man, your father, trustworthy. Now, what I have to tell you must be treated the same way. You must speak of it to no one."

"Not even Sebhot?"

Pepi considered this. "Not even Sebhot. Not yet." He leaned forward and put his elbows on his knees. "But send him to me, and I will explain matters." He looked expectantly at Imhotep, who nodded.

"If that is how it must be."

"It is. Your father and I and several others, whom I will not name, were called in to speak privately with the prince, as I have said. At that time few people knew much about the Sons of Atum. Their doings were confined to the lands close to Nubia, far south of here, and no one thought they were any more than a few local insurgents, malcontents like other such groups, averse to paying taxes to a distant ruler who did not share their religious beliefs." He made a gesture. "There are many such bands in the Two Lands, I regret to say. Some are no more than gangs of thugs. Here we are in a period of prosperity and peace, yet some people…" He shook his head. "But enough of that. I had heard of the Sons, but like everyone else I assumed they were no more than a gang." He scowled more deeply. "Prince Djoser gave us to understand that they were more, far more. They had been linked to politically motivated killings up and down the Nile, and their influence was growing among certain religious sects, who swore allegiance to them."

"To what end?"

Pepi gave him a grim look. "To the overthrow of the king and the establishment of one of their own as the ruler of our country."

14

But that…that's impossible."

"No, it isn't. Imhotep, think of a heap of sand. There are a few grains on top of the heap, but there are many more on the bottom."

Imhotep frowned. "Do you mean to say that the 'grains' on the bottom of the pile, by which you mean people, feel oppressed by the weight resting on them?"

"You can certainly look at it that way," said Pepi, nodding. "The Sons claim to speak for those who have no voice, who feel ignored by the king. But no matter. The point of what I wished to say is that Djoser wanted us all to be alert for suspicious activity. Signs of terrorism, you know…acts of violence, omens and portents, and so on."

"You, too, think the tattoos have something to do with the Sons, then?"

"I can't say for sure. It's possible; but again, it could also be merely a group of drinking friends vowing eternal friendship."

"I think it is more than that." He told Pepi of the soldiers who had visited the abattoir, warning of incidents involving the Sons, and of the disgruntled man on the ferry when Imhotep had gone to work on his father's tomb.

"Hmm. So, the news is trickling down to the general public now, eh?"

"Do you think…could this mean their activities are becoming more widespread?"

"Perhaps. We can only speculate. All I can say is that at that time, Djoser did not want the information to get out. It appears his thinking has changed. It could mean increased movement on the part of these terrorists."

Imhotep turned the information over in his heart. "Suppose…suppose you were wrong, and my father *did* tell someone?"

Pepi frowned. "Who would he tell? Your mother? Certainly not you or your brother."

"No…he would tell the person closest to him in business, the other person who was, like him, talking with customers and going to job sites and meeting a variety of people. The person he trusted, who knew more about the atelier's finances than anyone else."

"You speak of Ahmose."

"Yes. Suppose my father told Ahmose about the Sons. If Ahmose was involved with them, what would be his reaction? What would be *your* reaction, if you were Ahmose?"

Pepi stared steadily at him. "If I were Ahmose, and involved with the Sons of Atum, and if I knew that my employer would henceforth be on the lookout for behavior one could pin on the Sons, well…I might well seek to…I might wish to have him silenced."

The two stared at each other for long moments.

"Chancellor, what if Ahmose somehow engineered my father's death? After all, what do we know of it? Who else was there? Only Ahmose." *And Kagemni*, he thought. *And Kagemni! Yes, he was there as well!* But there was no time to pursue the thought, and he put it aside for later. "We know that my father was examining a wall when it suddenly fell on him. Ahmose claimed to have been injured in the accident…but we know he certainly wasn't hurt as badly as he claimed to be."

Pepi steepled his fingers. "We may be dealing with a conspiracy."

"You had better not say anything of this to Ahmose," said Imhotep. "It could put you in danger." He hoped Pepi hadn't said too much already, but there was nothing that could be done about that now.

Pepi nodded slowly. "You could be right. I will tread most carefully on this ground lest I cause a landslide, as the saying goes."

They gripped forearms, and Imhotep departed for work. His thoughts turned to the thin young man who had been trailing him. Was he a spy for the Sons of Atum? Or was his appearance only a coincidence?

The day was a blur of heat and work for Imhotep as he and the other apprentices labored over dripping haunches of meat. There was to be a huge banquet at the palace to honor some visiting dignitaries, and the day's quota of butchered meat needed to be doubled.

Excited by his early morning conversation with Pepi and more determined than ever to get to the truth of Kaneferw's death, Imhotep threw himself into the work, hoping that his diligence and determination would win approval from Ni-Ka-Re. At the end of the day Imhotep dragged himself home, too exhausted even to eat his supper. He collapsed into bed and knew nothing more until he was roused by Wabet the next morning.

"You have slept later than usual," the slave said. "I thought it prudent to rouse you."

"Oh, by the gods!" Imhotep stood up slowly. Every muscle in his body ached.

Wabet frowned. "I have just the thing for you, young sir," she said. She hurried downstairs to the main floor and by the time Imhotep had limped to the head of the stairs she was already climbing them, bearing a pot of unguent in her hands. Wabet made him sit on his bed while she rubbed the ointment into his flesh.

He began feeling better almost at once. "This stuff stinks, but it really does work."

"Yes, it's a good concoction."

Imhotep stood. His stiffness seemed to melt away. "Thank you, Wabet. Now I'd best be off." He sped downstairs so fast that he almost tripped over his feet.

As he came through the gate Ni-Ka-Re called to him from

the small work area where he kept accounts and records. A pile of shards covered with writing lay on a small table in front of him. "Where in Set's name have you been? I've been organizing the order for Ahmose's wedding. You're the best I have when it comes to reading and writing, so I'll need you to deliver it all to his house later. Take Tesh-Pa and Dhuti with you. Arrange the meat as Ahmose's cook directs you. She may ask you to assist with the serving. If so, tell her there will be an extra charge. If she does not, return here immediately."

"Yes, sir!" Thoroughly cheered, Imhotep turned to go.

Ni-Ka-Re frowned. "Hold. What's that terrible odor?"

"Odor? Oh, it's me. It's a salve I use to ease sore muscles."

Ni-Ka-Re wrinkled his nose. "It smells like river mud! Be sure you wipe it off before you deliver the meat, else the cook will think we're foisting spoiled food on her."

Somewhat chastened, Imhotep set to work.

Shortly before noon he, Tesh-Pa, and Dhuti—all three cleaned to the best of their ability—tottered through the streets toward the home of Ahmose, laden with baskets of freshly butchered meat wrapped in linen to prevent blood dripping.

Odji came to the door to admit them. "You'd best go around the side," he said, eyeing the baskets. They followed him down the side alleyway between Ahmose's home and the one next to it, into the courtyard kitchen where Ahmose's cook was fuming and cursing about the extra work she would have to do in order to feed all the guests.

Ahmose entered the kitchen, accompanied by an attractive but severe-looking woman. Judging by her clothes and jewelry, she was a person of some wealth. Ahmose was dressed in his finest clothing, with an intricate and beautiful golden pectoral collar around his neck. Imhotep was interested to see that he still wore a sling for his "broken" arm. *So, he is keeping up the imposture. I wonder why he bothers? For this woman's sake?*

Ahmose seemed to be in a fine mood. "Hello, Imhotep! Pay Cook no mind. She has many things to complain about. Or so she claims!" He looked fondly at the woman beside him. "This is my bride-to-be, Nodjnefer. She is seeing to the decoration of the house."

The apprentices inclined their heads. She stared rather stonily at them.

Tesh-Pa, looking at Ahmose, grinned. "Sir, you look most well turned out." Dhuti nudged Imhotep and they exchanged grins at Tesh-Pa's transparent attempt to ingratiate himself.

"How kind of you to say so." Ahmose looked the three up and down. "And you…"

Imhotep smiled. "At least we do not smell, if you require help serving."

"*I* damned well need the help!" The cook had come up behind them to inspect the bread. "Put that meat down and come back to the kitchen right away." She stalked off.

The butcher shop apprentices shared amused glances.

Ahmose scowled. "In Hathor's name, I don't know how I tolerate her insolence."

Nodjnefer spoke at last. "Her food is divine. Doubtless that is why," she said flatly.

Imhotep felt a surge of irritation. *Ahmose never had enough wealth to attract a noblewoman, as this Nodjnefer person seems to be… until recently. Nor could he have afforded to engage a cook. He certainly does seem to have improved his lot.*

He tamped down the anger. "Ahmose, Ni-Ka-Re bid me tell you that there would be extra charges for having us help."

Ahmose waved the fact away. "That's not a problem. Come. You are all still rather grubby." He led them to a lavatory, where they swiftly rubbed oil on themselves and used scrapers to remove it. A servant came with new linen loincloths for them. Feeling much cleaner, Imhotep returned with the others to the kitchen, where they surrendered themselves to the cook. Used to receiving the lash if they dawdled, the apprentices knew how to keep busy and unobtrusive, so before long the cook's spleen found other victims among the cringing kitchen staff.

A slave herded a pair of honking, outraged geese from the

street into the courtyard. He set to slaughtering and cleaning them faster than Imhotep would have believed possible and soon a cloud of plucked feathers surrounded him. Several ducks penned in a small enclosure to the side were also doubtless destined for the banquet table.

"You!"

Imhotep jumped.

"Are you deaf?" the cook demanded. "Get that bread sliced! Set out olive oil on the serving table! Our guests will soon arrive."

Imhotep stepped over to a table and began cutting the fresh loaves. As he watched, the cook slid a previously slaughtered goose into one of the ovens. The woman never missed a beat in her stream of invective toward her underlings.

"No, idiot!" she screamed at the perspiring Dhuti as he rubbed spices onto yet another goose. "More rosemary, *less* cumin!"

"Yes, mistress," he panted. "Your pardon, I have never worked in a kitchen before." Hastily he stuffed the carcass with bread, onions, and figs. Cook passed a critical eye over his handiwork and pronounced it fit for roasting. Into the oven it went.

Swearing all the while, Cook fussed with pots of butter and cheese, rejecting one of the containers of butter because it was rancid. Odji was dispatched to the marketplace to fetch another, followed by vituperation and curses such as Imhotep had never heard issue from a woman.

After slicing the bread, Imhotep carried a platter of it inside the house, relieved to be away from the furious cook.

The house was well fitted out for a celebration. Everywhere shallow bowls of oil lamps filled the rooms with a warm radiance that went well with the delightful cooking odors drifting in from outside. The wooden columns supporting the ceiling were wreathed in garlands of flowers. Incense censers stood on tripods in every room. Plain everyday wall mats had been exchanged for opulent linen tapestries decorated with scenes of the hunt and of life among the gods in the West. Comfortable pillows and mats were arranged in every room for the pleasure of the guests.

Imhotep followed Nodjnefer's nasal voice into the front room of the house, where other tables were heaped with flowers. Blossoms even hung from the walls. Nodjnefer stood in the middle of the room giving orders to several slaves while Ahmose, at one side, looked at a scroll.

Ahmose said, "We must remember that Chancellor Pepi can't eat onions because they come back on him, so—"

"Pardon, master," said Odji, coming up to him. "The musicians have arrived."

"Good. Have them set up where they'll be out of the way."

Odji bowed. Soon the sound of harps and flutes drifted through the house.

"Imhotep!" Ahmose called.

"Yes, sir?"

"We need more tables. Help set them up."

"At once."

Imhotep assisted with the placement of small tables near the sitting cushions. "Usually, you have two people to a table," said the slave overseeing the chore. "They'll put their plates there once they are served."

Imhotep's stomach liked the sound of that. "What sort of food?"

"Oh, the usual party fare. Chickpeas and lentils, fresh-cut lettuce, cucumbers, and onions. Figs, dates. Plus, bread. Meat, thanks to your butchery! And cheeses to go with them, and of course beer. *Lots of that.* The hot food, the goose and beef and so forth, won't be served until all the guests are here."

A flurry of activity at the doorway caught their attention. Ahmose said, "Our guests are beginning to arrive. I must greet them. Tesh-Pa, you and Dhuti may leave now. Take some food from the kitchen in payment for your efforts. Imhotep, you are well-spoken…I wish you to stay and assist with serving this evening."

Tesh-Pa and Dhuti shrugged at each other and departed. Imhotep, feeling a little uncomfortable, stood by, waiting to be told what to do as Ahmose hurried out.

"Ha!" Odji looked through into the entryway and scowled. "Chancellor Pepi. He always arrives early, eats everything in sight, and leaves late."

Imhotep watched in amusement as a young female slave named Thanasa met the old magistrate at the portal and guided him to a small table, on which had been set a tray with cones of scented ointment. Using a palm leaf, Thanasa scooped one of the cones off the tray. After greeting Ahmose and Nodjnefer, Pepi crouched down slightly, allowing the girl to place the cone firmly on the top of his wig. During the party, the balm would soften, melt, and drip down onto his robes, staining them yellow but releasing a delightful fragrance. Ahmose already had one such cone on his head. Sluggish waxy rivulets dripped down his face like oily perspiration.

"Well, we can talk about the festival later, Chancellor," he was saying. "Come, Thanasa, introduce our distinguished guest to a jug of wine. I have imported a special batch of Babylonian vintage for you, Chancellor."

"Indeed? It is my favorite. Lead me to it, girl."

"Yes, Chancellor," the girl said. "This way."

"Thank you, I'll be most pleased to make its acquaintance," said Pepi, following her into the next room.

Certainly, Ahmose shows no discomfort at having the chancellor here, Imhotep said to himself. Despite their recent conversation.

Other guests began arriving soon after Chancellor Pepi's entrance. For a while the slave girls were hard pressed to supply ointment cones in a timely fashion. Nodjnefer kept the slaves busy. This included Imhotep, who had no opportunity to speak with Pepi.

Gradually the influx of guests slowed to a trickle. The last person to show up was, to Imhotep's surprise, Ni-Ka-Re, who wore a rather out-of-style wig of thick wavy hair.

"Ah, dear brother!" said Nodjnefer, coming up to him and planting a kiss on his cheek. "A blessing on your night."

Imhotep's ears perked up. *Ni-Ka-Re is her brother? I did not think he came from money. Why would a man from a noble family be working in a butcher shop?*

Ni-Ka-Re grunted. "Thank you, my sister." He bent over for his ointment cone.

"Come, take food! We have roast goose, fresh bread…"

"I will do so."

The overseer approached Imhotep's table. As he did so Imhotep noticed that Ni-Ka-Re already smelled strongly of drink, and his eyes were red. "Well, well, young sir! You are surprised I am here?"

Imhotep ignored the taunt. "It is always good to see you, master."

"I daresay. Now I would very much like to see a jar of beer, so please excuse me."

Tired as he was, Imhotep had little time to rest; he and the slaves were kept busy dashing back and forth like ibexes, laden with plates of delicacies. It all smelled heavenly, and despite his exhaustion he was happy to be part of the festivities. He knew he'd get little enough sleep that night, but he was enjoying himself too much to care. It had been months since he had been at a party. In happier days, his father threw them often for his clients. But his mother, still mourning, would be attending no parties for many days to come.

With a sigh he thrust this sad thought out of his heart and concentrated on the gaiety around him. There was precious little joy to be had in the butcher shop and he meant to savor it as much as possible, even if he was present only as a servant.

15

As the jars of beer disappeared the level of conversation rose until people were nearly shouting to make themselves heard. The musicians in the main room were all but drowned out, but it didn't matter, as no one paid attention to them anyway. Everyone was smeared with melting ointment. All the furniture and most of the walls would need to be washed on the morrow. The fragrance of the flowers mingled with the scent of the ointment and the food, filling the air with delightful odors.

Toward the end of the meal, the musicians moved into the main room. Now dancing girls wearing jewels appeared, and lithe acrobats who twisted, jumped, and turned. The musicians handed out small tambourines and cymbals and encouraged the guests to join in by chanting, clapping, or playing the instruments.

The evening passed. Somehow Imhotep, by snatching a gulp of beer here or a swallow of food there, managed to keep awake and reasonably alert. Curious about the Babylonian wine that Pepi favored, he tried a mouthful, but it was not to his taste. Nor, he noticed, to most of the other guests, several of whom sampled the drink when it was offered to them but refused any more. Apparently only Pepi found it palatable. The chancellor drank steadily, becoming increasingly red-faced. He tried to place the cup down on the table before him. Imhotep, passing around a platter of bread, winced as Pepi almost missed his aim.

"You watch," said Odji as he brought in another steaming platter of sliced goose. "He'll be groping the girls next. Has a weakness for slave girls, does Pepi." He favored the chancellor with a murderous look.

Pepi, who was quite drunk now, had his gaze firmly fixed on

Thanasa as the scantily clad servant girl passed through with a plate of fruit. "I see what you mean," said Imhotep, embarrassed for the old man.

Without warning, Pepi lunged for Thanasa, knocking his table over. A small clay platter of half-eaten couscous crashed to the floor and broke.

All conversation stopped at the noise, and the music died away. Thanasa deftly dodged the drunken man and hurried gracefully out of the room, leaving Pepi swaying among the mess he'd made.

In the silence a shout of harsh laughter rang through the room.

"Hail to thee, Pepi," cried Ni-Ka-Re, lifting his jar of beer in salute. He laughed again. "I see you still favor the servants!"

Pepi, fists clenched, turned on him in a fury. "Shut your face, you ugly son of a slut!" he shouted, spraying spittle. Imhotep's eyes went wide. He would never have suspected the old man capable of harboring such venom. *Then again, alcohol will bring out inner demons.*

Ni-Ka-Re rose to his feet. Imhotep had watched the husky man drink five or six jars of beer. Intoxicated on his arrival, by now Ni-Ka-Re had to be as drunk as Pepi, if not more so. However, Ni-Ka-Re evidently had better self-control, for he showed little evidence of intoxication.

"What did you say, Chancellor?" he asked quietly. "What was that you called me?" Imhotep's heart chilled. There was a cold, dead gleam in Ni-Ka-Re's bloodshot eyes.

Nodjnefer sidled up to her brother. "Sit down. Sit *down!* You are disgracefully drunk," she said with a note of fear in her voice, as if she knew what her ill-tempered brother might do to the equally drunken Pepi.

Snarling, Ni-Ka-Re seemed about to say something, but she clutched at his tunic, whispering urgently in his ear.

She's probably reminding him that if he's stupid enough to assault Chancellor Pepi, who is well regarded at the king's court, there could be disastrous repercussions, Imhotep thought.

Ni-Ka-Re paused, still swaying on his feet. There was a strange light in his eyes as he turned toward the elderly chancellor. "Yes, well, it's a party, isn't it? And such things happen. Perhaps I have had a bit too much to drink. I crave your forgiveness."

"Think nothing of it," Pepi growled.

Nodjnefer, a look of exasperation on her face, went to the musicians, who stood frozen in the doorway to the room. "Play more loudly! It is time for dancing!" Obediently the instrumentalists struck up a cheerful, quick-tempo tune. Some of the guests did get up to dance.

Pepi, sneering at Ni-Ka-Re, turned his back on him and went for more delicacies.

Nodjnefer motioned for the slaves to remove the remains of the chancellor's plate. Imhotep began clearing a table, close enough to Nodjnefer and Ni-Ka-Re to hear them speaking.

"Now tell me," Nodjnefer said quietly to her brother. "What is your difficulty with the old man?"

Ni-Ka-Re's face twisted into a scowl. He spat expertly, if rudely, into a potted plant. "Forgive me, sister. There is no difficulty. I find myself weary. I shall be leaving now. I feel particularly tired of dried-up old officials." With dignity he stepped around Imhotep and left the room. Nodjnefer followed along in her brother's wake.

"Yes," said Pepi to the assembly at large, after Ahmose's wife-to-be and her brother had left the room. "There, you see? You see how Ni-Ka-Re flees at the sign of authority, like a common thug? That is all *he* is, a thug and a bully." He grunted, his anger having apparently evaporated as quickly as it had gathered. "Those who work for him know." He cast his gaze on Imhotep. "Would you not agree, son of Kaneferw?"

Imhotep, startled by the sudden turning of eyes toward him, blushed. "Uh, circumstances can bring out different sides of a person," he said, lamely. But Ahmose's cold gaze was on him as well and he didn't want to air any ill feelings.

Pepi snorted. "Ever the diplomatic one, you are. Well, the

hour grows late. I will have one more cup of wine, however."
He raised his hand for Thanasa, who glided warily over with a
small jug from which she refilled the chancellor's cup.

"A disgusting display of temper," Pepi said, taking a large
pull at the wine. "He is like an infant, squalling and—" He
choked.

Imhotep, standing nearby with an armload of platters,
looked up. Pepi clutched at his throat, half rising from his seat
before collapsing back into it. The goblet fell from his hand
and smashed on the floor. Pepi leaned to one side and vomited.
Staring at the dark red liquid pouring out of his mouth, Imhotep thought, *It's the mark of a good party.*

Pepi choked once more. To Imhotep's shock, he went into
convulsions. Guests clustered around, shouting. Nodjnefer
appeared from the entryway and pushed her way through to
the stricken man rolling on the floor in his own spew. At the
sight of him she shrieked. Several men knelt beside the chancellor, whose face had turned a horrible gray. Another woman
screamed. Then they all began screaming.

Nodjnefer took the old man's fouled hand as if to comfort
him. It seemed to work, because suddenly he ceased struggling.
He lay still, mouth agape, eyes staring up at the ceiling.

Nodjnefer's own eyes had gone wide and blank. She stared
uncomprehendingly at him for a few moments, then dropped
his hand as though burned. "By the gods, he is dead!"

Other guests crowded around. A man grabbed Pepi's hand,
frowning. He looked at the others. "It's true. He has gone to
the West." Slaves converged on the spot, pale-faced and shaken.

Ahmose came up behind Imhotep and grabbed his shoulder.
"Let's get the guests out of here." They began herding shocked
men and wailing women outside to the patio.

After this Imhotep returned to Pepi's body. "There's something—" he began to say, then broke off. A suspicion grew in
him. "Thanasa," he said, looking at the slave girl. "Fetch me a
duck from the pen outside, will you?"

She blinked stupidly at him. "A duck?" she managed.

"Yes, yes, in the name of Osiris, a *duck,* Thanasa! They weren't all slaughtered, and I need one. Now! Now!"

She scrambled to her feet and dashed outside. From the courtyard he heard the wailing of the women, their keening meant to accompany Pepi's newly departed spirit as it adjusted to its abrupt entry into its new existence. Taking no notice of the filth in which he knelt, Imhotep ran his hands over Pepi, sniffing him and prodding at his flesh. He knew from studying with Hau how to feel for the beat of a living heart; here, there was none. He had not really expected to find it.

"The...the d-duck," said Thanasa, returning with the bird. She stopped just short of the puddle of vomit surrounding Pepi's body.

"Well, give it here, then!" Imhotep said impatiently. She handed the duck to him. It flapped its wings, but he kept a firm grip on it.

"Now, get me that jug of wine he was drinking."

Thanasa quickly stepped back from the foul puddle and looked about for the serving jug from which she had poured Pepi's final drink. It stood on a table off to one side. She went to it.

"Pour some into a cup," Imhotep said. She did so and offered it to him.

He rose to his feet with the complaining duck in his hands. Carefully he forced the creature's beak open. "Now give the wine to the bird."

"Uh," she said. She was pale and seemed about to faint.

"Do as I say, please!" he said through gritted teeth, not wanting to speak harshly but knowing it was the only way to get her attention. "I have to see something. Pour the wine down the duck's throat."

The slave did as she was told. Wine splashed over Imhotep's already stained tunic, but some managed to get down the bird's gullet.

Within moments the bird, too, went into convulsions. After a few moments more, it stiffened and lay still in Imhotep's hands.

"Poisoned," he said grimly. Thanasa looked in horror at the cup of wine in her hand.

Chancellor Pepi had been murdered.

16

Ahmose stepped forward, scowling. "The royal investigator Weni-Ka lives nearby. I will send for him at once." Imhotep had not met Weni-Ka, but he had heard of him. The man belonged to a select group of officials who specialized in determining the facts behind unnatural deaths and other crimes. Their work was approved by the court as well as the Temple of Ptah.

Odji looked up at his master, clearly expecting to be delegated for this task. But Ahmose turned to Thanasa instead. "The house on the corner of the Bright Street and the Avenue of Palms. Do you know the one?"

"With the red gate. Yes, master, I know it."

"Summon Weni-Ka at once. Tell him…tell him Chancellor Pepi's dead." He glanced at Imhotep. "Possibly poisoned."

Imhotep bristled. *Possibly* poisoned? But he remained silent.

The girl nodded and sped into the night. Other servants made as if to begin clearing away the mess, but again Ahmose spoke.

"It would be best if we touched nothing. The investigator will want to examine the scene for clues. He may see something we have missed."

Imhotep stood staring down at the body. He felt light-headed and his vision swam. He had seen so much death lately! His father, Unas the butcher…and now Pepi. *Am I about to faint? It cannot be! I will not.*

The guests milled about, talking amongst themselves in low tones. No one seemed to have any idea what to do. Several of them prepared to depart.

"Hold," said one. "We may all be wanted for questioning." The others grumbled but made no further move to leave.

In the courtyard Nodjnefer and the other women were still wailing away. Their mourning made a discordant backdrop. The hired musicians and dancers hurriedly packed up their instruments and costumes and would have departed, but Ahmose bid them stay as well.

Imhotep was still feeling weak in the knees when Thanasa returned with the investigator in tow. Weni-Ka was obese, red-eyed, and rumpled, and appeared as if he had been asleep just minutes before. Barefoot, he wore a linen robe bearing traces of his last meal. Imhotep's nose wrinkled. Weni-Ka had apparently not cleaned himself in several days.

This fat, oily man with piggy eyes and two chins was a palace official? A solver of crimes, a pursuer of evildoers? The only thing even remotely interesting about him was the small monkey sitting on his shoulder. The creature's bright eyes looked everywhere, seemingly missing nothing.

"What happened here?" Weni-Ka rapped out. He had, Imhotep noticed, terrible teeth—some were missing and those remaining were no more than brown stumps.

Several guests began talking, but he held up his hand. "Not all at once, curse you!"

Ahmose cleared his throat. "We were having a party, sir. Chancellor Pepi drank some jugged wine. Apparently, it was poisoned, as my young associate Imhotep here seems to have proved." He nodded at Imhotep, who found himself the uncomfortable object of Weni-Ka's scrutiny.

"Proved how?" Weni-Ka barked at him.

As Imhotep explained about the duck Weni-Ka took the jug and sniffed at it. He lifted it up and let the monkey on his shoulder have a sniff too. The little creature recoiled. Weni-Ka grunted. "You may be right," he said grudgingly. "Very well, we shall have an investigation."

Several of the guests groaned. Weni-Ka, Imhotep knew, would want to talk to everyone present. Someone might have seen or heard something that would lead to the killer. The process would take time, and the hour was already late.

Pepi's killer—why, he is probably still here! Imhotep glanced around at the guests.

Weni-Ka stared distastefully at the well-to-do people in the room. "You'd all certainly want me to be thorough if it were a loved one of *yours* lying here dead." He didn't bother to hide his contempt. Turning to Ahmose, he said, "Send a messenger to the guardhouse at the main gate of the palace. I would be in your debt. Have him ask for my assistants, Panemma and Hama."

"Very well." Ahmose summoned another slave and sent him on his way.

Weni-Ka rubbed his nose. "I wish to examine the body," he said.

Imhotep watched as Weni-Ka bent to inspect Chancellor Pepi's corpse. He leaned closer over the vomit to sniff it. Imhotep's stomach lurched. "Wine," Weni-Ka said. He looked critically at the mess. "And much food."

"It was a banquet, after all," said Ahmose with some irony. He folded his arms. Hearing the grumbling of the other guests, he turned to Odji. "Our guests must be made comfortable while they are here," he murmured. "Arrange for their ease in the main room. Pillows, robes for those who wish them, and food and drink."

Odji bowed. "At once, master."

"Good, get those cattle out of here," Imhotep heard Weni-Ka mutter. Despite his shock at Weni-Ka's manner, Imhotep was intensely curious about how the man would proceed. He'd never been present at a crime investigation before, and certainly not one conducted by a man with a monkey on his shoulder. The creature wrung its tiny hands and chattered quietly as its master leaned over the corpse.

Weni-Ka reached up to scratch the monkey's chin. It closed its eyes in evident pleasure. "This man died after having taken one drink from his cup," Weni-Ka murmured to himself. "That means a fast-acting toxin. His face is raddled, and his throat is distended, which suggests his breathing was interrupted by the poison. There are several poisons that could cause the effects we see. And it couldn't have been in his wine earlier or he would have died that much sooner." He looked at Ahmose. "No one else drank the wine?"

"To my knowledge, a few people sampled it, but only Pepi favored it." He looked expectantly at Thanasa. "This one was serving."

Thanasa flushed. "Uh, yes! He probably had seven or eight cups."

Still on his knees beside the body, Weni-Ka rubbed his bristly chin. "Which argues that the killer was someone familiar with his tastes. Most households do not have much wine on hand. It's a rarity here in the Two Lands of Kemet."

Imhotep, watching, felt a growing respect for this disheveled man who was obviously a great deal cleverer than he looked.

Ahmose made a dismissive gesture. "Your pardon, but Pepi had traveled in Babylon and grew fond of the stuff while there."

Imhotep lifted his chin. "This is true. My family has known the chancellor for many years, and he often spoke of his fondness for Babylonian wine."

Weni-Ka nodded. "It was common knowledge, then, his liking for it?"

"Ye-es, sir. I would say so."

"I see. Was there anyone present this evening who might have had a grudge against this man?"

Ahmose pursed his lips. As if reluctantly, he said, "Odji, here, my slave, has often voiced his dislike for Chancellor Pepi."

Imhotep's heart went ice cold. He whirled around. Odji stood as though transfixed, the color draining out of his face. His jaw hung open in shock.

"Oh?" Weni-Ka levered himself slowly to his feet, grunting like a pig as he did.

Imhotep bit his lips, remembering the times Odji had spoken to him of his hatred for Pepi over his sister's treatment. Had the dislike festered long enough to have grown into an urge to kill? He stared wide-eyed at Odji.

Weni-Ka advanced on the trembling slave. "We will talk, you and I." To Ahmose, he said, "I require the use of a scribe."

Imhotep coughed. "I am a scribe, sir. I have acted as one in my father's atelier."

Weni-Ka skewered him with a disdainful look. "Thank you, but witnesses do not take their own notes."

Imhotep chewed his lips but said nothing. *He's right; I should have known that.*

"The house next door employs a scribe," said Ahmose. "Thanasa, fetch him." She trotted away.

Weni-Ka settled his bulk into a chair next to a small table. The monkey slid down his arm and sat on the table, staring at Imhotep. Imhotep in turn could not keep his eyes off the wry little creature. "She's very clever," he said in as friendly a tone as he could muster. "What's her name?"

"*His* name is Hukheru." The investigator's manner was neither friendly nor unfriendly. Both he and the monkey stared at Imhotep.

He bore their mutual scrutiny. At this relatively close distance he could catch the scent of Weni-Ka's decaying teeth. He clamped his jaw shut, praying to Horus that Weni-Ka would come no closer to him.

A few moments later a wispy old man with a pronounced squint arrived carrying a scribe's palette. "I am Sihathor," he said. If he was upset by the death of Chancellor Pepi, he showed no sign of it. Instead, he sank into a sitting position on a comfortable cushion in one corner of the room, moistened his ink cakes, and, selecting a piece of ostraca from among those in the basket he'd brought, sat with his reed stylus poised over it, looking inquiringly at Weni-Ka.

"An account of your presence here, please," said Weni-Ka to Odji.

Odji gave his name and repeated the same story he had told Imhotep—he and his sister, Noha, had been taken in a raid and sold to householders in Mennefer; he to Ahmose and she to Chancellor Pepi.

"I see," said Weni-Ka. "So, you are a domestic slave."

Odji nodded.

Weni-Ka frowned. "The scribe cannot *hear* a nod," he said. "Please speak your response."

"Your pardon. I mean, yes." Sihathor swiftly sketched symbols on the piece of pottery. Odji watched in fascination at the man's rapid strokes.

Weni-Ka caught his interest. "Can you read, boy?"

Odji started. "Y-yes, sir, I can read and write."

"Hmm. Unusual in a slave."

Imhotep glanced at Ahmose, who was surprised and angry to hear that his slave was literate. *I'm going to be in trouble when Odji reveals who's been teaching him.*

"Imhotep, here, has been teaching me without my master's knowledge."

"Ohhhh?" Weni-Ka gave Imhotep a sharp look. "I see. Well, we will get to *him* presently."

Imhotep swallowed. He said nothing but nodded his head once. He did not look at Ahmose.

Weni-Ka continued interviewing Odji. "And how comes it that a slave wishes to learn how to read and write?"

"I have vowed that I will not always be a slave." Odji lifted his chin.

Weni-Ka grunted. "Perhaps not; perhaps soon you will be a convicted felon."

"I did not kill him."

"Possibly; possibly not. We shall see. It has been claimed that you have spoken of your dislike for Pepi. Have you threatened him?"

"I—I never did."

"Yet he is dead, and apparently you are the only person here who bore him any enmity."

"I tell you that I did not kill him." Odji spoke with dignity.

Weni-Ka grunted. He turned to Imhotep.

"Why have you been teaching this slave things he does not need to know?"

"I saw nothing wrong with helping someone better himself."

Weni-Ka stared at him for such a long time that Imhotep began fidgeting. "You say your family has known Pepi for years."

"It's true."

"Give me an accounting of your recent doings, please."

As proudly as he could, Imhotep described his father's sudden and unexpected death, and his need to secure work. "And so, Ahmose was…kind enough to use his influence to find a position for me in the abattoir." He hated having to speak well of Ahmose and longed to voice his suspicions concerning the man's possible involvement with the Sons of Atum. This, however, was not the time to muddy the waters of a murder investigation.

Weni-Ka nodded to himself as Imhotep spoke. "I thought that you were something of a stranger to hard work."

One of the onlookers chuckled.

Imhotep went red. "How could you know that?"

Weni-Ka lifted a pudgy hand and waved it airily. "Even in this light I can see that your hands have new calluses. Also, I knew that you are the son of the architect Kaneferw, and would not be laboring in an abattoir were you not forced to do so."

Again Weni-Ka had proved that he might be gross of figure but his unappealing exterior masked an incisive mind. Imhotep found his initial dislike of him fading, shading into respect tinged with amusement at his own shortsightedness. His tense muscles relaxed a little.

Weni-Ka rubbed his chin in what Imhotep was coming to think of as a characteristic gesture. Hukheru copied the man's motions. Imhotep clamped his mouth shut to avoid laughing, but a small gasp escaped through his nose. Weni-Ka glared at him. "A man died here tonight, and died horribly, in front of many witnesses. If you have nothing further helpful to tell me, you may go."

Imhotep, face burning, turned to leave. Then something occurred to him. "Wait—I drank the wine shortly before Pepi had his final goblet of it."

"Ah! At last, some useful words pass your lips. How long before?"

Imhotep pondered the question. "I believe I was the last person to drink from the jug before Thanasa left the party to refill it and then returned," he said. "When she came back, Pepi called for more and she poured it for him. He drank...and..." He shrugged.

Weni-Ka looked at Ahmose. "I want the slave Thanasa!"

Thanasa had been out in the rear courtyard with the women. Now she came in and sat before Weni-Ka, trembling. After Sihathor wrote down her name, the investigator asked her to account for her actions that evening.

"It was my task to ensure that there were sufficient quantities of beer and wine," she said, pale but composed. "I made sure that the jugs were filled. I helped Cook prepare the food, and I supervised its serving." She said all this proudly.

"So, you gave the poisoned wine to Chancellor Pepi."

Thanasa faltered and her face grew pale. "Well, I, uh—yes." She pursed her lips. "I did."

"Did you add anything to the wine, either on your own or at the behest of another?"

She drew herself up. "I did not! I know he died from poison, but I had nothing to do with—"

Weni-Ka raised a hand to halt her protest. "How many times did you refill the wine jug?"

She bit her lips, thinking. "Three times, sir."

"Mmm-hmm. And Pepi died after the third refill, then?"

"That is correct."

"How long was it between the time you filled the jug for the second time and for the third?"

Thanasa's brow knit as she considered his question. "About long enough for half a torch to burn," she said.

"Bleeding sands!" Weni-Ka said. The girl stirred in dismay. He waved his hand in the air as if to dispel an unpleasant odor. "That's *plenty* of time for someone to pour poison into the storage amphora. By that time no one else was drinking the damned wine, is that correct?"

"Ye-es," said Thanasa. "Several people sampled it earlier but only Chancellor Pepi had a taste for it."

"As we have heard." Weni-Ka glanced at Imhotep. "This fellow corroborates your testimony."

Thanasa gawked at him. "Sir?"

"He agrees with your description of events!"

"Oh—oh yes, sir."

Weni-Ka cursed under his breath. "We've got a cold-hearted, beady-eyed snake on our hands. This killer timed his poisoning well. He waited to be sure no one else was drinking the wine. Then he added the toxin to the main jug, and it went from there directly to Pepi." He dug a finger into his ear, looked at what he found there, and flicked it away. "Damned lucky no one else had a swig from it first…that would have unmasked his plan, sure enough. Quite a risk he took there."

Cold-hearted indeed, thought Imhotep, beginning to sweat as the audacity of the killer's plot sank in. He and Thanasa exchanged silent glances. Off to one side, Odji stood, looking utterly miserable. Imhotep glanced at him. *Could he really have murdered Pepi? I cannot believe him capable of it. But Pepi had abused his sister…*

Hukheru the monkey scratched himself intimately.

"Where was the wine stored?" Weni-Ka demanded of Thanasa.

"In the cellar," she replied.

"And how is that accessed?"

"Across from the front hallway are stairs leading down."

"That is in the front of the house," he said.

"Yes," said Thanasa.

Imhotep thought he saw Weni-Ka's line of reasoning. He said, "But during the early part of the evening, Ahmose was at the doorway, receiving guests. I was nearby all that time. No one went into the basement."

Weni-Ka waved this aside. "The wine hadn't been poisoned then. Obviously. Our snake did it later, when more people were around, when it would be easy for him to slither off without being noticed." He thought for a moment. "Describe your activities at the beginning of the party," he said to Thanasa.

"Ahmose greeted the guests as they arrived, and I handed out unguent cones."

Weni-Ka glanced at Sihathor, who was writing impassively. "And after all the guests arrived?" he asked the girl. "What were you doing then?"

"I was busy serving food and jars of beer."

"Did *you* notice anyone going into the cellar?"

"N-no." She paused. "But a number of people did go toward the front of the house, because that's where the lavatory is."

His scowl darkened. "How many people?"

She fidgeted. "It...I—most of them, I suppose, at one time or another during the evening."

"You *suppose.*" He muttered a string of curses under his breath. Sihathor looked expectantly at him. "Don't write that, scribe." To Thanasa he said, "But you saw no one actually go into the cellar."

"Yes. I mean, no. I mean, I saw no one."

"And you didn't, either," he snapped at Imhotep, who jumped.

"No!"

"I...I did go down there myself, as I have told you," Thanasa said.

Weni-Ka sighed. "Did Pepi have any conflict with other guests tonight?"

Thanasa bit her lip. "He did have a dispute with Ni-Ka-Re."

The official listened closely as she described the confrontation between the abattoir's overseer and Pepi.

Imhotep saw the investigator's eyes glitter at this. Weni-Ka glanced at him questioningly. Imhotep shrugged. "It is as she says."

"*Then* what happened?"

She blew out her breath. "Then Ni-Ka-Re left the party."

"He left the house?"

"That's right. He was the first person to depart."

"Via the front door?"

"Yes."

Which…is near the cellar entrance, Imhotep thought, in dawning comprehension. *That would certainly rule Odji out as a suspect.* He sat back, hoping his satisfaction did not show.

The slave who had been sent to fetch Weni-Ka's colleagues stepped into the room, followed by two men. "I have returned with Panemma and Hama." Hama was a broad man with a squint to rival that of Sihathor. Panemma, tall and thin, lacked a finger on his left hand. Imhotep wondered how he had lost it.

"Ah. Good." Swiftly the investigator described the situation to them. "I want you to take statements from the other guests and household members." They nodded and left the room. "And you." He looked at Imhotep. "You were actually at Pepi's side when he died, were you not?"

"Well, more or less."

Weni-Ka grunted. "Tell me what happened."

Imhotep did his best to describe in detail the scene of Pepi's death, even though his gorge rose at the memory, and he even gagged once or twice during his discourse. Weni-Ka waited patiently for him to recover. "Yet you retained enough presence of mind to suspect poison and proved your supposition with the help of a duck. I will say, that was quick thinking, young sir. You have given me a good accounting. Perhaps too good an accounting." He gave Imhotep a narrow look. "That will do for now."

He turned to Sihathor and asked to see what the scribe had written. He was still examining the report when Panemma entered the room. He went straight to Weni-Ka and quietly spoke for a few moments in his ear.

"I see," said Weni-Ka, rising. "Where is he?"

"We kept him there."

"Let's have a look at him."

Imhotep and Thanasa exchanged wide-eyed glances. Imhotep shrugged and trailed along after the officials. They went to
a small enclosure behind the house, where Odji stood beside
a rude sleeping pallet that was no more than a sewn cloth pad
stuffed with straw. He turned wide, terrified eyes toward Weni-Ka. Then he caught sight of Imhotep.

"I did not do it! I don't know how it got there!"

"Be quiet, slave," said Weni-Ka. "How else is it to be explained? Show me," he said to his men.

Hama produced a small unguent pot. "This was inside the
pad." He handed it to Weni-Ka. "People think it's very clever to
hide things in their beds. It's always the first place to look. And
sure enough...all I had to do was reach inside. There it was."

Hama said, "And inside, this folded piece of papyrus."

Weni-Ka took it from him and unfolded it. Inside, Imhotep
saw, was a large quantity of powder, white with a yellowish
tinge.

17

His heart sank. *Is that the substance that killed Pepi?* He very much feared it was. From his studies with Hau, he was sure he recognized the powder, which looked fluffy with some grit in it.

Weni-Ka sniffed at the powder. "We'll have to have a healer in to tell us what this stuff is."

"I can tell you what it is," said Imhotep. "I have studied healing. It is spider lily. It's made from an infusion of crushed crinum bulbs. In Kush they use it in very small doses to treat certain maladies of the stomach."

"Oh. I see." Weni-Ka grinned, exposing his terrible teeth.

Imhotep ignored the sarcasm. "The plant is very rare north of the Second Cataract; in other words, anywhere in the Two Lands. There are other remedies that are cheaper, safer, and easier to procure, however, so healers rarely prescribe it."

Weni-Ka nodded. "Well, we will check on that. In the meantime, it comes from Kush, you say?"

"Most commonly."

"As does the slave, Odji." Weni-Ka nodded again. This time a grim smile split his face.

Imhotep stared at him. *By Thoth! I have sealed Odji's doom!*

"He spoke often of his hatred for Pepi," said Ahmose to Weni-Ka, with a shrug. "He claims that the chancellor mistreated his sister." He smiled. "Imhotep here will agree, I'm sure."

Imhotep kept his face composed. Ahmose now knew that Odji had been coming to Imhotep for lessons. Imhotep didn't know how that knowledge might translate to his treatment at the abattoir, but he was certain it wouldn't be to his benefit. Ahmose would find a way to punish him for having the temerity to teach Odji—his slave—anything at all that would elevate the youth in life.

"Is it so?" Weni-Ka demanded.

"It is so."

Ahmose sighed. "These stinking Kushites. I don't know why anyone would help them; they are so obviously inferior."

Imhotep flared inside but held his tongue.

Weni-Ka nodded without smiling. "He had the motive and the opportunity, and more of the very same poison used to kill Pepi has been found in his pallet." He stared at Sihathor the scribe without really seeming to see him. "I think we have all we need."

"Are you finished with me, sirs?" Sihathor looked up expectantly.

"I believe so. You have done well."

Sihathor bowed his head. "Here are all my notes." He handed a small heap of shards to Weni-Ka.

"Thank you for your time, scribe."

"You are most welcome. I will show myself out," Sihathor said with a yawn, and departed.

Weni-Ka had his assistants take Odji away. The slave protested his innocence with every step. Ahmose's guests likewise departed, in twos and threes to guard against depredations of wandering night-time ghosts.

Imhotep felt too low-spirited to want company. He threaded his way through streets and byways, unable to get his heart away from thoughts of Odji. The first time he had ever seen the slave, Odji had accompanied Ahmose to Kaneferw's atelier, carrying a basket full of architectural drawings and plans Ahmose had been working on.

Which reminded Imhotep of his own feelings of frustration and helplessness in the face of what had happened to him lately. *I will be more like Odji,* he thought, glancing up at the stars. Almost immediately came the conviction that Odji had not killed Chancellor Pepi. Though evidence and clues pointed toward that conclusion—the most damning of which was the discovery of the poison among his belongings—Imhotep still could not believe it.

Pepi had been murdered, though; there was no doubt in Imhotep's heart about that. Given his own dislike for Ni-Ka-Re, he was inclined to believe that the abattoir's overseer was somehow the responsible individual, save for the fact that he had already left Ahmose's house before Pepi died. He might still have engineered the death, but it was difficult to see how. That left Weni-Ka with only one credible suspect: Odji.

But why kill Pepi in the first place? Yes, perhaps personal enmity entered into it, but Imhotep felt certain that that was not the true motive for the chancellor's death.

No, there is something else, some other reason.

Home at last, he climbed the stairs to the rooftop where his mother and brother were already asleep. He settled onto his own sleeping pad with a sigh of relief and closed his eyes.

Moments later they snapped open.

Of course. Pepi *knew* something, something that could incriminate someone else guilty of a serious crime. He was killed for the knowledge that he possessed, or that someone *thought* he possessed.

And that knowledge, Imhotep realized with a chill, must have something to do with the Sons of Atum. The most logical conclusion might be that Ahmose believed Pepi was too close to some damning truth.

Odji simply wasn't a killer. Imhotep would stake his own life on that. The slave might despise Chancellor Pepi and hate the treatment his sister Noha received at Pepi's hands, but he was incapable of murder. His mouth twisted in a grimace. He knew what Weni-Ka would say about *that* little piece of insight. The investigator operated by dealing exclusively with what he could see, touch, and hear—and taste, given his disgusting personal hygiene, but Imhotep dismissed this bit of levity.

Odji has been set up, he said to himself. As a slave, no one would take his claim of innocence seriously, particularly when his master had been so willing to throw him to the hyenas.

Imhotep's thoughts returned to Pepi. He remembered the last time he had seen the man before the party. Then he recalled his feeling that he had been shadowed, by the thin-faced young man with the tattooed foot, on his way to Pepi's home.

Yes, that had to be it. He *had* been followed…and overheard as he discussed his suspicions about Ahmose with the chancellor. Imhotep's eyes narrowed. Ahmose was too clever and devious to be caught trailing Imhotep, so doubtless the thin-faced man was some Son of Atum who had been given the job and had listened outside while he and Pepi talked about the Sons and his father and Ahmose. The listener must have known that Imhotep, like Pepi, was getting close to some truth.

He swallowed. *That means I could be the next target.* The thought made gooseflesh crawl about on his limbs. Would he be killed? When would it happen? Where? *Probably not right away…not so soon after Pepi's death. No, they'll wait for the excitement to die down, probably for days, maybe even weeks.* He examined that thought from every angle, satisfying himself that he was right and that it was not just his own fearful thinking.

Could he possibly be wrong about all this? Again, could he simply be rushing to a conclusion with little evidence to support it?

He didn't think so. His father had certainly died; the atelier's finances were in serious disrepair; Ahmose had certainly lied about his arm being broken; some men certainly bore tattoos; the Sons of Atum were certainly becoming more active in the Two Lands, particularly in Mennefer and the surrounding regions. How did it all fit together?

Despair soaked through him. What could he, one person, do about the plot he felt sure must be developing all around him even now?

Lord Thoth, guide me. Tell me what I must do. I am one very small person against many powerful doers of violence. But this night the ibis-headed god was silent, and there were no signs among the stars, though Imhotep lay awake for a long time seeking one.

❧

Wabet had to rouse him the next morning. Another package of freshly caught fish had appeared by the door overnight, which Wabet said she'd make into a fine evening meal. Gratified by the gift but still sodden with sleep, Imhotep made his way slowly through Mennefer to the abattoir, scuffing his sandals in the dirt, feeling as though his eyes were full of grit and his head full of mud. He tried to stay alert to his surroundings as he went about his work, but it was difficult because his lack of sleep made him slow, stupid, and cross. Even so, he managed to avoid the lash.

At noon while he took his meal, despite his thick-headedness, he noticed Kagemni staring coldly at him. These days, the man always seemed to be lurking somewhere nearby.

With a shock Imhotep came fully awake. He now knew who would officiate at his death. There would be no poison, no toppling walls, for him. Most likely it would be an "accident" here at work, where there were so many sharp implements used to slice and carve, and so many opportunities for one to lose one's footing amid the bloody mud of the ground.

Yes—one slip, and a man carrying a knife could well blunder into another man, "accidentally" inflicting a serious, if not mortal, wound.

And Kagemni will say, Oh, I am sorry, it was all so unfortunate. I will say many prayers to speed his ka to the Beautiful West. What a shame, that family has endured so much tragedy... Imhotep's lips twisted in grim amusement and for the remainder of the day he was doubly careful about what he did and who was nearby.

Before long, one thought and one thought only spun its web in his heart: *There has to be someone I can talk to about this. There must be...*

When he returned to his home late that afternoon, he had the germ of an idea. He sought out Sebhot. His younger brother might not have the experience of years, but he was practical and level-headed.

Imhotep found him up on the roof, polishing senet throw-sticks, jackal-headed and carved from ebony. "I want to go see Prince Djoser," Imhotep said.

Sebhot stared at him for several moments without speaking. "You're mad," he said at last. "Do you want to get yourself thrown into prison?"

"Why? For what? There's a conspiracy going on with the Sons of Atum, Seb."

"What?" Sebhot exclaimed, eyes wide. "By Osiris, Tep, what are you talking about?"

Imhotep drew a shaky breath, then went on to explain about the tattoos and his suspicions concerning their father's death. "Pepi knew. I talked to him about it. He didn't want me to say anything to you; he was going to fill you in himself, but then he—he died. But the tattoos are proof."

Sebhot stared at him for a few moments. "Well, maybe. You've got some facts, and some inferences and suspicions, but you haven't really got *proof.* This is a lot to take in. Listen, Tep, I'm as anxious as you are to find out what really happened to Father, but—"

"Then this is what we must do! You agree that the tattoos are real?"

"Well, yes, if you say so. I know you don't make things up."

"And that they indicate a conspiracy?"

Sebhot growled. "Look, there's evidence in that direction, but again: you can't say you have any proof." He settled down on a stool beside his sleeping pad. "Follow my reasoning, brother. Everything started when Father was killed, right?"

"Yes, of course, we—"

"Bear with me! Father is killed…Ahmose has a broken arm that turns out not to be as badly hurt as he said."

"Well, exactly! He—"

"Patience. He's a manipulative person, is this not so? He told me that he was using the injury as a means of getting some sympathy from potential patrons…to get more work for Father's atelier."

Imhotep's shoulders slumped. "You never told me this before."

"When have I had a chance? You are gone in the morning, and when you come home at night, you're usually so exhausted that you fall asleep right after eating."

"But the money! The bills, Father's debts—"

"Yes, yes. And we know that Pepi found discrepancies. Ahmose said that they were the result of him being distracted and upset after Father's death and making some errors as he wrote entries into the ledgers. Remember, he said that the accounts were in disarray after Lord Horemheb withdrew his commission, and that he had to put extra work in to make them reconcile."

"Well, then, why was Ahmose at Father's tomb that day, when I went there to complete the painting?"

"You said he said he wanted a word with you in private."

"Well, yes, that's what he *said*. But I don't believe him."

Sebhot sighed. "Imhotep, I don't believe him either, but if you go to Djoser with a pile of half-crazed suspicions, he'll toss you out as quick as the snap of a crocodile."

"By Set's neck wattles! What of Pepi? Someone *killed* him, Seb. The man is dead. Just after I was speaking to him about my suspicions about Ahmose. I'm convinced someone followed me to his home and listened outside while we spoke." And he told Sebhot about the thin-faced young man with the shifty look and the tattooed foot.

Sebhot considered the information. "Well, it is true that Pepi is dead...but it's clear to the authorities, and me, that Odji killed him in revenge for the way Pepi was treating his sister."

"I refuse to believe it."

Sebhot looked steadily at him. "Anyone can kill, given the right circumstances. And no one can say what the right circumstances are for anyone else." He shrugged. "What would it take for *you* to kill someone? Probably not the same thing it would take for me to do it."

"But Odji—"

"You are not Odji, and neither am I. We don't know what he was thinking or feeling. Look at the evidence! They even found more of the spider lily in his bed, right? And, by Thoth, it was you who identified it."

"Well, yes."

Sebhot spread his hands. "There you are. I say, don't go to Djoser. At best he will laugh at you. At worst..." He shrugged.

"But Pepi said that Djoser told him that he should be notified in case of suspicious activities."

Sebhot put a hand on Imhotep's arm. "Listen, brother...no one has a higher regard for you than I. If there's any truth to the idea that there are people of exceptional intelligence in the world, geniuses, then I think you probably are one. I believe you're going to be a great man one day."

"Seb, I don't know what to say—"

"Say that you won't go to Djoser until you have hard facts at your disposal. I am trying to save you from making a fool of yourself in front of the very person you most need to help you in your career as a healer, architect, whatever it is you want to be. Royal patronage, Imhotep. You know this as well as I do. Look how well placed we are. We are in a well-to-do household. Or we *were*. We might as easily have been tending flocks now, had Father been a farmer, say, or a herdsman."

Imhotep looked down at the floor. "I know how fortunate we are," he muttered.

"We've had life served to us like dates on a plate, brother." Sebhot picked up a throw-stick and began polishing it. "You are clever and resourceful, you are well educated and come from a good family, and we are known to the king and the prince. You have been growing close to Meresankh. Are we not blessed among men? We have the opportunity to be of real service to the Two Lands with the atelier's work. Do you want to throw that away?"

Imhotep sighed. "What you say is true. But to be of service requires a stable...government. Stability, Seb. The Sons would rob us of that. My first loyalty is to the Two Lands, as you say. And that's why I must see Djoser."

It was Sebhot's turn to sigh. "Well, I see I cannot talk you out of it. Not that I really thought I could. You are a stubborn, headstrong person."

Imhotep slapped his brother's arm. "And you love me as your brother."

Sebhot grinned wryly. "When will you seek Djoser out?"

"Tomorrow, after work. I know I can get into the palace… Father's name will open the doors for me; plus, the prince knows me."

"Pray he isn't too occupied with affairs of state to see you."

"I shall be praying to Thoth every step of the way."

The next morning, Imhotep left for work earlier than usual, impelled by his excitement about his upcoming audience with Djoser. The eastern sky, hidden by the buildings around him, had not given more than a feeble gray hint of the forthcoming arrival of the sun god's boat.

At the abattoir the day progressed with agonizing slowness. Imhotep impatiently accomplished his tasks at work while reviewing in his heart the things he wished to say to Djoser. All the while, however, he did his best to remain alert to what was going on around him. Pepi's death had made him jumpy, and he kept a careful eye on Ni-Ka-Re and Kagemni while he labored.

They know that I helped Weni-Ka identify the poison used to kill Pepi…they must consider me more of a threat to them now. Sebhot would say I am being overly cautious, but I know foul plans are being hatched around me. I must be vigilant and cautious.

18

After work, he cleaned himself off as well as he could, knowing that he'd need to be at least minimally presentable if he intended on seeing Djoser. Usually he would have waited until he got home, but now, having brought with him a small stone jug of oil and a fresh tunic, he oiled and scraped his skin and donned the clean garment. Then he set off for the palace, following the Street of the King, which passed near the abattoir.

At this time of day, the city's buildings glowed with an orange-red light as Lord Re's boat slipped nearer and nearer the horizon, turning from a blazing circle in the sky to a sullen red ball floating to earth. The Street of the King led nearly due west. He imagined that he was walking directly into the fiery globe, where he would see his father and all those others who had already passed into the Beautiful West.

He wondered what it was like there. With something of an effort to restrict his thoughts to the business at hand, he kept his senses alert.

He doubled back occasionally in case someone was following him, taking a cross street to the left or right, then turning east at the next junction, running back in the direction from which he had come, and then returning to the Street of the King somewhat farther back.

He did this two times but didn't see anyone trailing him. If anyone happened to be shadowing him, they were either farther back or else were better at following than he was at detecting them.

The third time was different.

He had just turned the corner back onto the Street of the King when he saw two men in front of him. He had not previously noticed them…and one was Kagemni. He was arguing with his companion. Imhotep stiffened. The companion was the same thin-faced, shifty-eyed man who had followed him before.

Imhotep ducked back into the cross street. His heart had somehow seemed to climb up into his throat.

"I tell you, he was just there!"

"Well, he isn't there now, Kagemni," said the other man in a thin drawl.

He sounds like a Theban; they speak slowly in that manner. Imhotep crept closer to the intersection, taking care to stay back. A passerby glanced incuriously at him, and Imhotep flashed a weak grin.

Kagemni and the Theban man moved farther off along the Street of the King.

Well, 'he' is me, no doubt about that. Now what should I do? Let them trail me to the palace? No…that isn't a good idea. They'd only be waiting for me when I came out.

He puzzled about it for a while without stepping out into the Street of the King. *Well, why should I stay on this street? There are other ways to get to the palace. I'll just take another route.*

With a brisk nod to himself, he turned around. Headed north now, he followed the intersecting street, itself little more than an alleyway twisting through a residential neighborhood.

His determination, strong before, had hardened like a sun-baked rock. If Kagemni and this other shifty-looking individual were interested in his doings and whereabouts, there must indeed be some sort of conspiracy operating in Mennefer. At the very least, Imhotep knew himself to be in personal danger. Ahmose might not have killed Pepi, but the odds were excellent that he knew who did. Imhotep had no intention of being the next victim.

He loped along, dodging children playing in the dirt, pedestrians, and wandering dogs. From behind he heard a disturbance: voices raised in dispute. He glanced back. It was the thin-faced man arguing with a pedestrian with whom he had collided. The man saw Imhotep looking at him and made as though to chase after him, but the other man grabbed him by the shoulder.

"See here, you, you made me drop my bread, and then you trod upon it! What is to be done about that?"

"To the demons with you and your bread!" snarled the Theban.

Imhotep didn't wait to hear more. Apparently, they were onto his scheme of taking an alternate route. *This fellow must be smarter than he looks. If only I could avoid the streets. But I'd have to be able to fly above the buildings like a bird, if I were to—wait!*

With a brief thank-you to Thoth, who was part bird and must have put the idea into his heart, Imhotep dodged into another side-street, little more than a winding passageway. Blessing his long, strong, thin legs for once (like those of an ibis, Thoth-in-his-heart commented), Imhotep scrambled onto a wall beside the lowest building of those crowded along the alley. Then he reached up and, panting, dragged himself onto the structure's flat roof.

Prior to working at the abattoir, he would not have been strong enough to accomplish the feat. Though he was still lean, the muscles of his arms and legs were now strong and taut.

Rising to his feet, he looked around. From here he could see across much of the city, because almost no other buildings were taller than this one except for the palace and some temples. Maze-like on street level, up here the city looked like nothing so much as a series of white flat-topped stepping stones leading toward his destination. *If I'm careful and choose my path wisely, I can probably make it to the palace on rooftops alone without ever having to use the street. So, let's see Hatchet-Face and Kagemni follow me up here.*

He set off at once toward the palace, which glimmered in the west. It was by far the most majestic building in the royal complex, with a surrounding wall and temples clustered around.

The hour was still too early for most families to be preparing for sleep. Many rooftops, therefore, were untenanted. Imhotep wasn't the only person to be making use of this aerial roadway, but he was probably the biggest if not the oldest. As a child he had taken dares from his friends to jump from one roof to another across a wider or narrower gap. He'd never been foolish enough to attempt some of the longer leaps, but now he put fear behind him in the face of his urgent need to see Djoser.

He scanned the rooftops ahead, intending to avoid those that looked to be in disrepair and those occupied by people. His progress toward the royal precincts, though indirect and slower than it would have been on the streets, was nevertheless steady.

Ahead the rooftops were closer together, indicating an older, more thickly settled section of Mennefer. He made good progress here. Then, while he ran lightly toward the far edge of a roof, a head popped up above the wall. A woman was climbing an outside staircase to the rooftop holding a basket of dates. She saw Imhotep running toward her and screamed.

"No, it's all right! I'm simply heading for the palace!" But the startled woman screamed again. *I'll have to go around.* Imhotep dodged to one side, increased his speed, and leaped for the adjacent roof. It did no good; the woman continued to shriek behind him.

By the king's beard! He dropped to his knees at the far end of the roof, took hold of the edge, and swung himself out. He landed hard, near a group of playing children, who gaped open-mouthed at him.

"It's hide and seek," he said, grinning as he passed. "Don't tell anyone you saw me!" The woman's cries faded in the distance.

Nearby, another outside staircase led to a roof. He took the steps two at a time. Cautiously peering over the edge in the direction from which he'd come, he saw no signs of pursuit. He scrambled up and continued, making sure to be more careful.

The afternoon light grew redder as the sun dropped into the west, nearly dead ahead. It dazzled Imhotep, forcing him to squint as he made his way along the rooftops. Suddenly he came to a gap across which he could not jump. It was a plaza, a small marketplace, through which people hurried toward home as the day waned. He muttered a curse and was about to drop down to the ground when he saw a palace guard saunter into the plaza, exchanging greetings with the citizens.

A stroke of luck! I'll talk to him, tell him what I know of the Sons of Atum, and ask him to take me to see Djoser. All the guards will be on alert for information about the Sons.

He was about to rise when the Theban ran into the plaza, headed straight for the guard. Imhotep froze once more, flattening himself on the roof. Thin Face spoke to the guard, waving his arms.

Imhotep chewed his lips. *I'd wager that he's saying the same thing I would say, except that he's giving that guard* my *description, and saying that I'm the terrorist!*

Thinking sour thoughts, he waited for Thin Face to be done spreading lies so that he could climb down from the roof and go on his way.

He was close enough to see the two men but couldn't hear what was being said between them. The guard listened to Thin Face, frowning, then said something short and turned away. He marched out of the plaza toward the palace. Thin Face watched him go, a nasty smile spreading across his face. Imhotep ground his teeth. Thin Face then left the plaza as well.

Imhotep climbed down from the roof on the side opposite the plaza. No one saw him drop into the alley. He walked as casually as he could to the end of the street and looked out into the plaza. People crossed it going this way and that, but of the Theban and the guard there was no sign.

Imhotep sighed and resumed his walk toward the palace. *Well, the day wanes…people will be heading up to their rooftops now, so I have probably gone as far that way as I can. I don't have much farther to go, though. I'll be at the palace before it's completely dark.*

Without really thinking about it, he touched the amulet at his throat for protection.

As he hurried through the streets, he rehearsed what he was going to say to Djoser. He had no worries that the prince would not know him; Imhotep had met him once or twice in company with his father. He remembered Djoser being imperious, but less arrogant than other royal officials Imhotep had encountered. Unlike them, Djoser had nothing to prove to anyone.

No, the trick here would be to get in to see Djoser at all. With activity by the Sons of Atum becoming a major concern in Mennefer, the palace would be doubly on guard against possible infiltrators.

He smiled a grim smile. Well, there was nothing for it but to take the ibex by the horns.

Ahead now, past the temples, lay an open space. Beyond this stretched the niched wall surrounding the king's palace. Beside it sat a single-story mud-brick building: the guardhouse. This had been whitewashed to make it match the wall and the grandeur of the palace, but its plain appearance contrasted sharply with the hundreds of niches that had been built into the wall itself, most of them containing altars or statues of various gods. Citizens could stop here at all hours of the day to address a prayer to their favorite deity.

Imhotep had just set foot in the plaza when he saw a man enter from the east side, away to his right: Kagemni, like an evil spirit come out of the night. Instantly Imhotep faded back into the shadows of the street from which he had just come.

Now what was he to do? He cursed his luck. Now he'd have to try the guardhouse at the main gate on the far side. He backtracked and set off to go around the large plaza. Finding his way blocked by a temple, he fumed as he backtracked further until he could gain the rooftops once more. They wouldn't take him all the way to the royal precincts, but by keeping aloft he should be able to see if Kagemni and the other man were nearby. If he saw no sign of them, he'd make a break for the guardhouse and hope he could talk his way in before his foes arrived.

Moving as quietly as he could, Imhotep threaded his way along the rooftops. This route was less safe than before; many roofs had people on them now, and he had to go far out of his way to avoid being accosted.

Fortunately, the night was yet moonless. Despite being nervous about wandering spirits, even though there were relatively few to be encountered in the city itself, Imhotep took this as a good sign; Thoth's home being the Moon, this was the god's way of helping him.

By keeping to shadows as much as possible, Imhotep got to within a short distance of the palace. At last, however, he came to a place where he would once more have to take to the streets. The problem here was that he wasn't adjacent to a street. Below lay a garden, obviously belonging to a rich man, because it was filled with acacia trees. Judging the distance to the nearest tree as best he could, Imhotep took a breath and made ready to jump. His palms were damp with sweat. This was exactly the sort of thing he had never loved doing as a young boy, when his friends made sport by jumping from branch to branch or from rooftops to branches. Imhotep had always hung back. Now he had no choice, but he felt more confident because of his new strength. He crouched and leapt.

There was a terrifying moment of hanging free in space, when he was certain he had misjudged the target and would crash to the ground, rousing the household.

Then his hands slapped bark and he grabbed for all he was worth. His legs swung free, but he scrambled up and saw that he was a scant distance from the ground. He blew out his breath in relief and dropped into a bed of flowers.

Like a ghost himself he sped across the garden, keeping a wary eye on the house to his right. Gaining the wall on the far side, he clambered up and over. The street was below. He wasn't sure which one it was, but he knew by the stars what direction to take. He was mere moments from the palace, which explained this expensive garden: doubtless this was the home of a nobleman.

None of that mattered now. He was almost at his goal. *I've done it; I'm free!*

Ahead the street opened out and he saw the plaza. It seemed that he'd been trying to get to it for years. The niches of the vast wall showed alternate bands of white, which he knew were stone, and black, which were deep shadowy niches.

Ignoring the wall, Imhotep marched up to the guardhouse. A guard standing at the door was facing the opposite direction and did not see him coming. He wore a leather helmet, a tunic bearing a black stripe, and carried a gleaming copper axe. A short sword hung from a leather belt around his waist.

Suddenly Imhotep was seized from behind. A weight crashed down on his head as a skin full of beer was poured over him. Another blow brought him to the threshold of unconsciousness, but somehow, he managed to hold on for a few moments, during which he saw that his captors were Kagemni and the man with the hatchet face.

"Hold, you there," called the guard. He walked heavily toward the trio.

Imhotep could not speak. Blackness closed in around him as he heard Kagemni say, "Good evening, honored sir! Please excuse us. Our friend has had too much to drink, and he decided he wanted a word with the prince!" Kagemni and his companion laughed.

The guard grinned. "Oh, aye, that happens often. Many people think they have better ideas on how to run the city and the kingdom! You'd best get him home."

"We will."

At that point, darkness claimed Imhotep and he knew no more.

19

He awoke slowly, aware at first only of a terrible headache and that someone had hold of his feet and legs. Other rough hands grasped his armpits. He was being carried somewhere. The smell of fish and stale beer was so strong that he gagged.

"Hear that?" someone said. "He's awake."

Kagemni? Imhotep opened his eyes but could see nothing. The rough feel of fabric over his face told him there was a sack or a bag over his head. Apparently, it had been recently used to carry catfish or perch to market.

Another voice laughed. *That's Thin Face.* Imhotep groaned. *What happened to me?* His aching head bumped on something, and he gasped in pain.

"We'll see him home, all right."

The pain cleared his thoughts a little. He remembered approaching the guard, then being grabbed, struck, and soaked with beer.

Kagemni and Thin Face caught up with me. He tried to move but found his arms and legs bound with cords. He began perspiring. Kagemni's next words did nothing to console him.

"Yes, home…to the Beautiful West!" He laughed coarsely.

"Stop wiggling, you, or I'll clout you good." Thin Face, who was at his head end, shook Imhotep's shoulders.

Imhotep ceased his struggles. He tried to concentrate on the outside world in hopes that he could determine where he was being taken, but he could tell little. Depending on how long he'd been unconscious, he could be almost anywhere in Mennefer—or out of it.

Probably not too far…they wouldn't want to be seen carrying me. Just then he heard the unmistakable sound of water, and the next thing he knew his captors were splashing through a small stream. *I am probably south of the main part of the city, somewhere along the river. Some fisherman probably used this sack, and there aren't many streams inside the city.* As though to confirm his deduction, the call of an owl came faintly to him. *You hardly ever hear one in Mennefer itself. We're definitely away from it. And it is still night.*

Now the question was, what were they going to do with him? His imagination conjured up several unpleasant possibilities. Fortunately, the uncomfortable ride didn't last much longer. Soon Imhotep was lifted and flung onto a flat surface.

He cried out in pain and received a kick.

Kagemni said, "No, let the meddling fool squawk all he wants." He laughed. "No one will hear him out here."

Imhotep spoke for the first time. "Who are you? What do you want with me?"

Kagemni snarled, "As if you don't know who we are."

"He doesn't know that…" There was more, but it was whispered, and Imhotep couldn't catch it.

Kagemni spoke again. "Well, we don't know what he knows and what he doesn't know, but we'll soon find out." His voice grew louder as he walked closer to where Imhotep lay on the floor. "And it won't be pleasant. You wait here, boy. We've got to decide how to proceed with you."

"The prince will be looking for me."

Both men laughed at this. "He might, indeed, did he but know where you were. As it happens, he doesn't know and never will."

Imhotep heard footsteps receding, then the sound of a door closing.

He frowned and set to work struggling with his bonds. The ones on his wrists were tight, but they were only dried vines, and he had room inside the sack to bring his hands up to his face. He attacked the bonds with his teeth and before very long had chewed through enough of them to pull them apart with his new strength. After that it was but the work of a few moments to free his feet, and then to force his way out of the woven bag, spitting out bits of plant fiber that had got caught in his teeth.

He lay on his back, gasping relatively fresh air in darkness, recovering his strength. Above him in the walls were the tall, narrow ventilation slots found in many homes, too small for him to squeeze through.

The room took up the entire floor space of the building, apparently, for there was only one door, and ventilation openings in the other three walls. To judge by the light coming through the openings from outside, the day was waning. Twilight was on the land, and Nut would soon spread her cloak of night over the Two Lands.

There was nothing else in the room other than a tall, covered basket at the opposite end from the door.

Propped up on his elbows, Imhotep gazed at this and was about to get to his feet to investigate when the door was flung open, and three men entered. It took Imhotep a moment to realize that the man with Kagemni and Thin Face was Ahmose.

"You managed to free yourself, I see," said Ahmose. "Well, it won't matter."

There couldn't be any doubt now. Imhotep didn't bother to beg for mercy.

"You killed my father."

Ahmose chuckled. "A wall killed your father."

"You engineered it, you…you—"

Ahmose shook his head. "You can prove nothing."

Thin Face took a step forward, his hand lifted to strike Imhotep, but Ahmose gripped his arm. "There's no need for that, Mereruka."

"He trusted you," Imhotep said.

"Which made it easier for me."

Imhotep knew he was being taunted. With a supreme effort he withheld the curses filling his mouth. His rage had the unexpected side effect of clearing his heart. Slowly he arranged his limbs, sitting cross-legged as though he were about to act as a scribe, taking notes.

"How did you do it, Ahmose?" he asked. "Did you weaken the wall beforehand?"

Ahmose looked surprised. "Clever, very clever. Yes, that is what we did." Here he glanced at Kagemni. "Our foreman here arranged for the other workers to be at the far end of the site while your father and I were inspecting the wall. It was sufficiently weakened that he could push it over easily."

"And your injury, your 'broken' arm…also arranged, of course."

Ahmose shrugged. "It would have seemed odd if I sustained no harm. As it happened, Kagemni hit me with a rock."

"But not too hard." Imhotep's eyes narrowed as Kagemni grinned.

"No, not too hard."

"And you killed Pepi."

Ahmose looked startled. "You guessed that?"

"Of course." It was Imhotep's turn to shrug. "It all fits. These two jackals trailed me, heard me talking to Pepi…and told you about it."

"Well, the old man was getting too close to the truth. Like you."

Mereruka spoke. "In any case, a slave killed Pepi. That Odji…because Pepi had been playing with his sister." He grinned. "She's a pretty thing."

"Restrain yourself, friend," said Ahmose. "There will be plenty of time for that later."

"Yes," said Imhotep. "First you have to kill me."

"Oh, *we* won't kill you, you meddling whelp." Ahmose nodded to Kagemni, who approached the basket at the other end of the room. With a muffled exclamation, Mereruka backed out of the room, and even Ahmose retreated a pace.

Imhotep knew what was inside the basket even before Kagemni tipped it over and ran for the door.

"We won't kill you, but *that* will."

Out of the basket slithered a full-grown red, spitting cobra.

Though the room was growing dim as daylight faded, Imhotep recognized the snake at once. There wasn't a single person in Mennefer who would not have known it, for it was one of the most dangerous creatures living in the Red Land, the end-less desert wastes surrounding the narrow belt of fertile Black Lands bracketing the Nile.

The cobra's bite was poisonous enough to kill a grown man in less time than he could count to five hundred. But it was universally feared and avoided more because of its ability to spit its venom, seeking to blind prey or attackers by aiming for the eyes.

Imhotep knew better than to attract the snake's attention by frantic movements to escape, but he had never been so terrified in his life.

He had seen blind beggars around the city. Milky-eyed, some of them, their sight gradually blocked by a sickness that spread a cloudy coating over their eyes. Or perhaps an unlucky stone-cutter struck the rock carelessly, getting chips in his eyes as a result. Others were blind from birth and had never known the glory of light and color that most people took for granted.

But there were also those who had come unexpectedly upon a spitting cobra in the wild and had not shielded their eyes in time to avoid the creature's venom.

I've got to cover my eyes lest I be blinded. But if I do, how can I watch the snake? He stared in fascinated horror as the snake slowly slithered out of its basket. Its tongue flicked in and out. It hadn't noticed him yet. In other circumstances he would have thought it a beautiful animal: bright red ochre in color, with a broad black throat band and teardrop-shaped markings under its glittering black eyes. But its colors were considerably grayed out in the dimness of the room, and it roused an almost unrea-soning fear in him.

If I cover my eyes, I'll be blundering around the room; the snake will attack and bite me. Cold sweat rolled down his torso. *And yet if I wait too long, darkness will cloak its movements and I won't be able to see it at all. I must do something very soon.* He willed himself to remain still while he went over everything he knew about snakes.

First, and most important: snakes rarely attacked unless they felt threatened. He himself had captured venomous snakes several times by moving very slowly, not making any sudden moves until he was able to grasp the creature behind its head so that it wouldn't bite him. Such risk-taking was common among the children of Mennefer, most of whom were expert snake-catchers.

But all the snakes he had caught this way had been small. This one was full grown, at least as long as his arm. Adult spitting cobras were nocturnal, whereas immature animals were active during the day. This snake was awake and ready for its nightly hunt. It would be fast and alert. Normally preferring toads and frogs, it would be happy to get mice or birds, or even other snakes.

It wouldn't want Imhotep for dinner, but it wouldn't hesitate to attack if he alarmed it. *Thoth, please help me remain calm. I am your humble servant pleading for your mercy now.*

He began to move, slowly. The snake instantly halted its exploration of the far end of the room. Facing him, it lifted its front end off the ground a little, weaving back and forth. There was just enough light left for Imhotep to see it flicking its tongue.

Alert—yes, it certainly was alert. He chewed his lips. *I must be more so.* Moving even more slowly, he lowered his hands to his tunic. There was, he recalled, a small rip over his left leg. His questing fingers found it and he set to work tearing a strip to use to shield his eyes if necessary.

Imhotep knew he didn't dare throw the stool at the snake; that would serve only to anger it and goad it into an attack Imhotep would not survive. The temptation was strong, but he resisted it. *I am not an old woman, to be terrified by a squeaking mouse running around the room.*

Watching the snake slip across the floor in the gloom, Imhotep used his foot to move the stool closer to the wall under a window slot. In one motion he stepped up on the stool and jumped. His heart leaped as his hands grasped the sides of the narrow opening. He drew himself up and stuck his head outside, bracing his feet on the wall. He inhaled cool night air, taking it deep into his lungs. The scent of dried mud came to his nostrils. For now, though, that information did him no good.

The sky outside was sprinkled with the first stars of night. The snake would not be able to reach this high…but he could not squeeze through the slot. He tried again and again, abrading his skin, but it was no use, even coated as he was with his own sweat. His younger, skinnier self might have managed the task, but he had grown too big to fit through the opening.

He remained where he was, clinging partway up the wall. It was probably safer than being on the floor, but even if it was, he wouldn't be able to stay up here indefinitely. Somehow, he had to find a way to escape.

Hanging there by his hands, which even now were beginning to ache, Imhotep leaned his head out into the night once more. *It's so frustrating…this end of me is out but the rest of me is in. What am I going to do? All I have is a strip of linen, my amulet, and the stool.*

He blinked. *And…the snake.*

Oh, blessed Thoth! An idea had popped into his heart. It was crazy, dangerous—terribly dangerous.

But he could see no other path.

Breathing continuous prayers to Thoth, Imhotep slowly let himself down from the wall. He stood quietly, watching the snake questing around its new environment. Very soon he would not be able to see it.

The only way to get out of this room was to capture the snake. It was far and away the largest one he had ever tried to catch. In a way that was good: the thing would remain visible longer in the darkened room, when a smaller reptile would be invisible. Perspiration slowly coursed down his body.

A year or so ago during a festival he had been wandering around the marketplace with Sebhot when their attention had been captured by a snake-handler surrounded by a crowd of onlookers. Imhotep remembered what the man had done, but he had never attempted it himself. Still, the tactic should work. He remembered questioning the man about his method after the show. The explanation had seemed simple enough.

But that was during daylight, with a torpid snake made slow and logy by the hot sun. Also, the handler had said that his snake was well-fed, and generally even-tempered in the first place.

This snake was fully awake and wary of possible foes. It was probably also hungry, and therefore irritable.

Yet I have no choice.

Clenching the torn piece of linen between his teeth, he stripped off the remainder of his tunic, leaving himself naked but for a loincloth. He wrapped the fabric several times around his left hand. With the other hand he took off his amulet and carefully secured it to the tunic, clenching the thong to keep it in position over his knuckles. The amulet would simulate eyes, he hoped; the eyes of the threatening creature his left hand had now become.

The snake watched with its beady black gaze. Imhotep prayed to Thoth that the creature wasn't clever enough to understand the subterfuge he was attempting.

He slowly settled into a squat and began to sway gently back and forth.

For some time, the cobra remained motionless, watching. Then, attracted by his rhythmic movement, it glided forward, approaching him cautiously. Its tongue flicked.

Now Imhotep began humming, as if he were crooning a lullaby. Very slowly he extended his arms. His legs began to shake from the strain of maintaining a crouch. With his arms spread as though he wanted to embrace the snake, he began making slow circular movements with his left hand.

The snake watched, never blinking. Its attention was fully on his disguised left hand.

Now for the most dangerous part of the plan.

Barely moving, Imhotep brought his right hand in toward the snake. He imagined that it was as small and as innocuous as an ant and moving more slowly than a worm. *I am so peaceful, so harmless…like a tiny minnow under the water, or a moth floating through the night looking for a flower. How could I ever appear dangerous? I am a turtle basking on a sunny old log, no thought of hurting anyone, dozing my life away in the sun. I am so sleepy, calm, and quiet...*

While his legs screamed to be relieved of their cramped position, he moved his left hand back and forth, back and forth, as slowly as a cloud drifting across the sky. His right hand crept closer.

He prayed for strength and courage, knowing he had only one chance to succeed. Otherwise, an agonizing death awaited him.

He had to be ready for failure, though. If he missed, he would have to protect his eyes with the rag clenched in his teeth. He would fling himself back and pray to all the gods that the snake would not attack.

He knew it was a forlorn hope.

Sweat trickled into his eyes but he did not dare shake his head to fling it away. He blinked fiercely. Attracted by even that faint movement, the cobra turned its beady black eyes toward him.

It was within an arm's length of him. He moved his left hand a little more energetically, not much, just enough to capture the snake's attention once more. He found himself unable now to hum...his throat was too dry, and he dared not cough.

He didn't want to do what he had to do. Again he thought: *I have no choice. Thoth, watch over me!*

He moved his left hand sharply. The cobra put out its hood, and he knew it was about to strike. He moved his hand again and the snake buried its fangs in the linen wrapping. Imhotep flinched, but they could not penetrate it. He grabbed the snake under the head while its fangs were caught in the cloth. It could not reach far enough back to bite him, but it was strong and frightened. He was amazed at how powerful it was. It flailed about, slamming its muscular body into his legs. It urinated and defecated on him, but he'd been ready for that so paid its filth no mind. The punishment it inflicted with its muscular body was worse, like a bad beating.

He knew he wouldn't be able to hold the enraged, terrified creature for more than another few moments.

He positioned himself to one side of the door. To attract his captors, he cried out in fear, fear that was only partially simulated. At the same time, he kicked the stool over. It clattered along the floor and fetched up against the wall with a thump. He cried out again.

The snake whipped and hissed, growing increasingly enraged. *Thoth, give me strength!* From outside he heard a muffled exclamation. Mereruka said, "That didn't take long, did it?"

Imhotep heard Ahmose say, "Be careful, you fool!"

The door swung open, and Mereruka stuck his head into the room, looking around cautiously. Imhotep thrust the snake at him. The maddened reptile, seeing a potential threat come within range, struck out, burying its fangs in the man's narrow face.

Mereruka screamed and fell back, staggering and clawing at his cheek.

Imhotep immediately followed him out, still holding the cobra, which was whipping around and hissing.

"What happened, Mereruka? By Horus *what happened?* Why did—" Kagemni broke off as he saw Imhotep step out of the hovel. "Gods!" Mereruka lay on the ground, yammering in pain and fear.

Kagemni recoiled, real terror in his eyes. With triumph surging in his veins, Imhotep flung the twisting cobra at him and was gratified by the burly foreman's shriek of fear.

There was no sign of Ahmose, and Imhotep took no time to look for him. *Doubtless the coward fled at the first sign of trouble.* He raced off blindly into the darkness, clad only in his loincloth, trusting to the stars to orient him. Behind him the wailing voices of Kagemni and Mereruka died in the distance.

Weni-Ka will be interested to learn of those two...though by the time he arrests them they may already be standing for their judgment at the Scale of Ma'at, sent there by my cobra. May the Eater of Souls take them!

Following the odor of mud, he trotted toward the bank

of the Nile. *Now, am I south of Mennefer or to the north of it?* He hastened toward the shore, alert to pursuit by his captors or to assault by a night-flying demon. He lacked his protective amulet now; he had dropped it during the confusion.

He topped a low rise and saw the Nile ahead of him, forming a broad band running across the land. About halfway between his position and the shore he spied a man running.

Ahmose. He rejected the idea that the fleeing figure could be anyone else. Though he was unarmed, Imhotep immediately set out to follow his father's murderous First Assistant. On the one hand he wanted to remain to see his plan to its end, but he knew he had to follow Ahmose.

20

He almost wished he still had the snake, but in his present state of fury he felt more than capable of dealing with Ahmose on his own.

Down at the shore, Ahmose turned left and hurried along with Imhotep shadowing him and doing his best to keep low so as not to be seen. But Ahmose never looked back. Ahead of Ahmose, Imhotep saw something lying on the riverbank. *A crocodile! Well, I'm happy to have another animal do my work for me this night.*

But it wasn't one of the scaly monsters. It was a long, low reed boat. Ahmose dragged it down to the water and pushed it in. Imhotep, flattening himself into the mud along the river, ground his teeth. *He was all ready to make a quick getaway. A clever snake in his own right. But where is he going?*

The boat slid out into the water. Imhotep, seeing his quarry escaping, chewed his lips in frustration. He glanced up at the glittering stars that spangled the night. No moon... He growled and walked to the water, then in until it was up to his thighs, praying that Ahmose would not look back and spot his pale body against the darker background of the river and the shore. Imhotep dove quietly into the Nile and swam after Ahmose's boat.

Imhotep was a good swimmer, but as Ahmose's boat pulled ahead, he wasn't sure how long he would be able to keep up. Fortunately, Ahmose seemed to be headed straight across to the western shore. The Nile was not terribly wide at this point, so Imhotep pursued him without much concern other than for river-dwelling predators like crocodiles or hippos. Now that it was night, however, there probably wasn't much to be afraid of.

Probably.

Where is he going? Does he have other confederates over there?

Imhotep kept as low in the water as he could, letting Ahmose get far enough ahead of him that he had little fear of being seen.

Close to the opposite shore, Ahmose angled his boat to the left, heading upstream to the south. Wondering, Imhotep went ashore and followed on land, keeping up as best he could along the riverbank. Ahmose drew ahead of him, but not by much.

Buildings appeared on the opposite side of the river. At last Imhotep knew where he was. *We approach Mennefer. But why on the western shore? Here is only the City of the Dead, tombs… He cannot mean to go there.*

Apparently, however, he did. Ahmose grounded the boat not far from the ferry landing, which was deserted at this hour. Dripping wet and shivering in the cool air, Imhotep trailed the First Assistant as he made his way up toward the ranked tombs.

Imhotep's flesh crawled at the proximity of so many dead, but he refused to give in to fear. Ahmose obviously knew exactly where he was going.

As he passed a familiar spur of rock, Imhotep gasped in understanding. *He is going to my father's tomb! But why?*

Dread and fury rippled through him. How dare this insect be anywhere near the resting place of the man he had murdered?

Ahead of him, Ahmose had reached Kaneferw's small monument. Now he pulled something from his tunic and bent over on the ground. The sounds of rock striking rock came to Imhotep through the quiet night air. Light flared: Ahmose had struck a torch. Jamming it into the ground, he yanked the tomb's door open.

Shocked to his core, Imhotep struggled to restrain himself. The desecration revolted him, but he knew he had to find out what Ahmose was doing.

He shuddered as Ahmose pushed his way inside. Imhotep crept forward. Muffled sounds came from within, like stone grinding on stone.

His eyes went wide. *He is opening my father's sepulcher!*

Sickened, Imhotep eased forward.

Now Ahmose appeared at the door of the tomb. In his arms he bore several linen sacks. *The thief is robbing Father's tomb.*

It was more than he could bear. Ahmose dumped the sacks on the ground, then went back into the tomb. Imhotep seized a stone and crept forward. Positioning himself to one side of the door where he would not be seen, he stood waiting in the darkness.

Inside he heard more heavy grinding and scraping noises. *If he moved Father's coffin before, now he is moving it back.* He clutched the stone in his hand. *What could he possibly be doing? There is nothing in there aside from what we left as offerings to help Father during his journey to the West. There is little gold, little silver…What is he after?*

Presently Ahmose came out once more, bearing another armload of heavily laden sacks. After setting them down, he grabbed hold of the tomb door and swung it shut, head down with the effort. He looked up and saw Imhotep, who had been standing behind the door. His eyes grew wide.

Imhotep grinned at him. "Blessings of the night to you." He brought the rock down on Ahmose's head. Ahmose dropped to the ground without so much as a squeak.

Imhotep stood over the First Assistant's unconscious form, breathing heavily. For a moment he was sorely tempted to take the rock and smash in Ahmose's skull, but only for a moment. Imhotep looked through the sacks Ahmose had taken from the tomb. As he had expected, they were full of the goods that had been provided for Kaneferw's journey to the Beautiful West.

He scowled and tossed the stone to one side. It clattered away in the darkness. *Prince Djoser will want to speak with this insect. As will Weni-Ka.* He tore Ahmose's tunic into strips and used them to bind him. Then he sat down to wait for daylight.

"What I really wanted to do, of course, was to run to the palace, but I didn't want to waste time explaining my story to the guards, and I hated the idea that somehow Ahmose might escape if I left him alone for any length of time. Instead, I decided I would wait until the City of the Dead's first visitors of the day arrived to pay their respects to their departed and have them fetch someone in authority."

Imhotep sat in a comfortable room in the royal palace, sipping a mug of beer and helping himself to dainties from a silver plate. His wounds and contusions had been seen to, and despite being short on sleep, he felt better than he had in many weeks. He had done his best to explain where the house in which he had been held captive was located, and guardsmen had been dispatched to find it.

Prince Djoser shook his head in admiration. "By Ptah! I wish I could have seen Ahmose's face when he saw you standing there."

"He didn't have much time to react before I hit him." Imhotep chuckled.

"You did the right thing." Djoser grew stern. "Tomb robbing is a serious crime. Ahmose will be very fortunate if the king does not condemn him to death."

"He knows a great deal about the Sons of Atum, though. I'm sure he'll be willing to trade information for his life. If not him, then perhaps Kagemni or Mereruka, assuming they survive being bitten by that cobra."

Djoser looked up as a servant approached him and whispered in his ear.

"Ah! Send them in at once."

The servant inclined his head and hurried out.

"The guards have returned."

Before he could say anything else, three beefy men at arms bearing swords and daggers clanked into the room. They knelt and extended their right arms in salute.

Djoser waved an impatient hand. "Yes, yes, honor to you and all that. What of those men?"

"The one called Mereruka was already dead by the time we located the house. The man Kagemni expired before we guards got him halfway back to the palace."

"Mmm. Very well, thank you, captain. See that the corpses are thrown to the crocodiles."

Imhotep bit his lips. A horrible fate—not for the two terrorists, who were already dead from cobra venom, but for their spirits. Without proper burial they would wander the red desert lands for eternity, angry and dangerous.

The guard's face remained impassive. "It shall be as you say, Your Majesty." He paused.

"Yes, captain?"

The captain of the guards crooked a finger to one of his men, who came forward with a linen sack. "We found this in a small shack behind the house in which Imhotep was incarcerated." He handed it to Djoser, who opened the sack.

From within Djoser drew forth a shining gold pectoral necklace, such as a man of means would wear on formal occasions.

Imhotep straightened. "That—that looks like my father's."

"Examine it." Djoser put it in Imhotep's hands.

"Yes…here is a small scratch on the back. He'd dropped it, you see. As fortune would have it, the blemish wasn't visible from the front." He looked at the prince. "We put this in his tomb."

Djoser inclined his head. "I am sorry that it has been profaned by those jackals, but we will see to it that priests visit your father's tomb to consecrate it after it is set to rights."

"Thank you, my lord."

To the guard, Djoser said, "And thank *you*, captain. Well done."

The guard extended his arm once more before rising and marching with his men from the room.

Imhotep sat fingering the gorgeous pectoral, saddened that Ahmose, whom Kaneferw had trusted, had so casually betrayed that trust by violating the tomb's sanctity, using it for a repository of goods purchased with money embezzled from the atelier's coffers. Ahmose had readily admitted his deeds under none-too-gentle questioning by the palace guards, saying that he meant to retrieve the goods before the tomb was sealed.

At least we know now that Father was not the profligate and irrespon-

sible man we feared he was, Imhotep thought, and sent a blessing to Kaneferw's memory. *His heart will weigh well against the feather of Ma'at.*

Djoser was saying something about Kagemni and Mereruka. "At least we still have Ahmose. And rest assured, my friend, he *will* be made to talk about others he knows in the Sons of Atum."

If Ahmose didn't talk, Imhotep knew, he'd suffer the same fate as his henchmen: eternal exile from the Beautiful West.

"They've been clever," Djoser said, "with this system of tattoos. We're inspecting all our prisoners to see if any of them have similar ones. We have learned that the Sons are arranged in small groups, with no group knowing all the members of others. Yes, a very clever arrangement, but we have cracked it now."

At Djoser's insistence, Imhotep spent the rest of the night in a sumptuous guest room. To his surprise he fell asleep quickly and did not wake until after dawn, when a servant roused him, saying that Djoser wished to see him.

He was ushered into the prince's presence, where, to his astonishment, he found Sebhot and his mother awaiting him. They both looked perfectly calm and composed, sitting at the morning meal with Djoser.

"Ah, Imhotep. Join us." The prince extended a hand. Imhotep restrained a grin at his brother's expression as he and Djoser clasped arms like longtime friends. Djoser must have caught Sebhot's look as well, because he favored Imhotep with the briefest of winks. "Your mother has told me of your difficulties following Kaneferw's death." Djoser frowned. "I wish to say that I am most sorry about his passing. He was a good man, and we valued his work. Of course, we all expected you to follow him in the business."

Imhotep squirmed in his seat. Was there to be pressure from *everyone* on him to become an architect? One did not lightly defy the expectations of royalty. "Yes, well—"

Djoser waved a hand. "I also know that you had been about

to depart on an adventure down the river when your father
died. I envy you."

"Wh-what?"

"I am not free to do anything that would take me away from
my duties here in Mennefer." Djoser smiled rather sadly. "So,
you see, I know something of how you felt about having to go
to work in the butcher shop."

"I had no choice, Honored One. There are debts, they must
be paid—"

"Indeed." Djoser reached into a basket sitting on the floor
beside his seat. "I can do something about that, at least."
He drew forth another pectoral, this one even grander than
Kaneferw's. "Ahmose had bought this, intending to give it to
his bride-to-be, Nodjnefer. Naturally, she will not now wish to
wed a tomb-robber and murderer. We will make suitable rec-
ompense to her, but we felt that it would be appropriate to give
this to your family." He handed it to Ankh-kherdu, who gasped
as she took it in her hands.

Djoser smiled. "It should pay off all your debts, allow you
to repair your father's tomb, and stock it with new offerings."

"I have...no words for your generosity, Honored One."
Kherry appeared to want to say more, but her voice choked off
and tears welled in her eyes.

"Needless to say, you won't be working at the abattoir any
longer," said Djoser, scowling. "It pains me deeply to think that
we have had such scoundrels in our very midst, defiling the
meat we serve in the palace."

"But not everyone working there was involved," said Imhotep, thinking of Dhuti and Snefru and Tesh-Pa and the other
apprentices.

"I understand that. We will discuss with the other workers
the possibility of organizing a new establishment that will supply our needs."

"Oh, that's good. Thank you, Honored One."

Djoser inclined his head. "It is my duty to see to the well-
being of the king's subjects." When he lifted his head he smiled

at Imhotep. "You're an intelligent and resourceful young man. Your father spoke very highly of you and your skills."

"He—he did?"

"Yes. He said that you had a number of interesting ideas about building and architecture." Djoser stroked his chin. "I am at liberty to reveal something about our plans for the city and the realm in the coming years. There will be a need for architects of vision and accomplishment."

Imhotep blinked. "I am hardly accomplished, lord. I have helped my father, but—"

"You do not realize that working with the famous Kaneferw places you ahead of many older practitioners of your art. He was respected by my brother the king, Imhotep. Quite well respected."

Imhotep swallowed. The image of the three-tiered step pyramid he had drawn flashed into his heart for a moment, and he wondered if Djoser would find the design interesting.

"What I wish to say is simply this," Djoser said. "You will take your voyage. You've earned it, Thoth knows!"

Imhotep blinked again at the mention of the god's name. Could Thoth have something to do with all this? Was he somehow speaking through the prince?

Djoser continued: "When you return, you will resume your studies here, at the palace, in the Temple of Ptah with the learned ones. We will work together, you and I. I feel that there is greatness in you, that you are favored by the gods." He grinned. "And who am I to argue with the gods?"

21

Just over a week later, Imhotep stood once more at the stone quay in Ankhtowe, at the southern end of Mennefer. Below, the Nile slapped the stone, murmuring wetly. A few paces away a group of sailors was piling goods into a boat rocking on the river's gentle swell, overseen by the bearded, sweating captain. "Hoy, hoy, hoy, you worthless hyenas! Step lively!"

Kherry eyed the man with distaste. To Imhotep she said, "Are you sure you want to subject yourself to life on the river for the coming year?"

His mother and brother were there to see him off, along with Hau the healer, Odji and his sister Noha, and several of the abattoir's former apprentices.

Imhotep sighed in frustration. "Mother, not in front of my friends!"

"But he's so gruff and unrefined."

"After Kagemni, this man is as delicate as a kitten, I promise you."

Tesh-Pa, standing beside Kherry, agreed. "Worry not! Your son is well able to handle himself." He lifted his hand, still bandaged from when Imhotep had broken his finger. Following Ni-Ka-Re's arrest, Tesh-Pa had been put in charge of the abattoir. "Imhotep, by the time you return from your voyage next year in the season of heat, we will have the abattoir well under control."

"I'm looking forward to celebrating your success." Imhotep clasped the other's forearm.

Snefru hit him on the arm. "It wouldn't have happened without you, Tep."

"That's right," said Dhuti. "We owe you much."

"So do my sister and I," Odji said, stepping forward. "Thanks to you, I now have a job and can support myself as well as Noha." Imhotep had secured his old job at the abattoir for the former slave after petitioning Djoser to free the boy and his sister in the wake of Ahmose's arrest.

Imhotep laughed, rubbing his biceps, which ached after Snefru's friendly punch. "I simply did what I was led to do by Thoth. If you wish to repay me, be honest in business and avoid trouble."

"That we will, that we will."

Imhotep's attention was taken by a running figure approaching from the far end of the pier. His heart leaped: Meresankh! He had feared that she would not be able to get away from the bakery in time to see him off.

The girl threw herself into his arms, to the amusement of the onlookers. Imhotep didn't care. She hugged him hard.

"Oof! You are much stronger than you look," he said, grinning.

"Lugging heavy trays of bread all day can make a girl strong," she said with a laugh, tossing her hair back.

"Imhotep!" A deeply tanned youth stood up in the boat.

"Thuya!"

The sailor grinned. "Aye. The ewer near you; can you bring that aboard?"

"Oh." *Speaking of strength!* Imhotep looked at it. It was exactly the size and shape of the one that he had been unable to move on his own during his father's funeral. And doubtless it was full of olive oil, making it even heavier. He stepped over to it and lifted it. Heavy, yes, very—but not, he thought, beyond his new strength. Though still thin he had new muscles now, crossing his arms and legs like tough ropes. *I have something to thank Ahmose for after all.* "Of course, Thuya." Conscious of Meresankh's admiring gaze, he hoisted the heavy ewer and with a grunt of effort stepped carefully with it onto the deck of the boat, set it down, then climbed back up on the quay. He embraced Kherry. "Farewell for now, Mother. I will have many tales for you when I am back from my journey."

"Then travel safely, arrive with joy, and return with honor."

He leaned over to kiss her. Facing his younger brother, he said, "Look after things, Sebhot. Stay away from the senet table!"

Sebhot put on a look of mock hurt. "You wound me, brother." Then he grinned. "I have a confession to make. You remember the fish and ducks and so on that have been showing up at our door?"

"Of course. Have you found out who is sending them?"

"Yes. It was me."

"What? *You?*"

Sebhot grinned sheepishly. "Yes, me. I have been taking my senet game down to the river where the fishermen and hunters meet in the morning and playing with them."

"Seb, you've been fleecing them!"

"Well, no, I've been careful to lose once in a while…but they pay their debts in fish and ducks, and I hired a boy to bring them to our house, making sure he would say nothing to identify me."

Imhotep shook his head in mock disapproval. "You will become a gambler if you are not careful, my brother."

"I already am one, Tep!" Sebhot laughed. "But you leave now… Be well, my brother. Luck, luck, luck!"

"Thank you, Seb. I promise, when I return, we will discuss this senet obsession of yours." He turned at last to Meresankh and took her in his arms once more. "Also, when I return…" he said.

Her eyes were shining. "I will send prayers to Thoth each day for your safety and happiness," she said.

"And I, for yours." He quickly turned away lest his eyes well with tears. He blinked furiously as he stepped down once more into the boat. Thuya was chalking a glyph on the ewer.

"That's the last one, my friend. We depart at once."

"Aye, sir!" Imhotep grinned. Biting his lips in excitement, he closed his eyes and addressed another thank you to ibis-headed Thoth for making the journey possible. In moments they'd be casting off, heading south toward—well, toward who knew what, really?

ACKNOWLEDGMENTS

Thanks are due to the many people who have read versions of this book over the years, but especially to Grace, to the endlessly patient and encouraging Val Nieman, and to Jaynie Royal and Pam van Dyk, also without whom.